the Hope *of* Christmas Past

A DICKENS OF A CHRISTMAS NOVEL
BY LAURA ROLLINS

ALSO BY LAURA ROLLINS

Lockhart Regency Romance

Courting Miss Penelope—available at LauraRollins.com

Wager for a Lady's Hand

Lily for my Enemy

A Heart in the Balance

A Farewell Kiss

A Well-Kept Promise

A Dickens of a Christmas

The Hope of Christmas Past

The Joy of Christmas Present

The Peace of Christmas Yet to Come

Copyright © 2020 by Laura Rollins

All rights reserved.

No part of this book may be reproduced in any form or by any electronic or mechanical means, including information storage and retrieval systems, without written permission from the author, except for the use of brief quotations in a book review.

NOTE FROM THE AUTHOR

Some time ago, the thought came to me to create a trilogy based on Charles Dickens's *A Christmas Carol*. However, in making one book become three stories, a single fact became immediately clear. This would not be a retelling in the truest sense of the word.

This is not a book about a grumpy old man who is visited by spirits in the middle of the night and awakes the next day a better individual.

Instead, I decided to take the essence of the three spirits and write one story around each of them. I wanted to take the messages told by the Ghost of Christmas Past, the Ghost of Christmas Present, and the Ghost of Christmas Yet to Come and explore the lessons and ideas they present.

That being said, many of the characters first imagined by Charles Dickens make cameo appearances here and there, though I have taken some liberties to aid in telling these stories.

I believe it is worth mentioning that some of the holiday terms we now use to reference the Christmas season were either not used in Regency times, used in slightly different ways, or used to mean slightly different things. Unfortunately, many resources were contradictory on this point—in those cases, I deferred to Dickens's *A Christmas Carol* and the complete works of Jane Austen.

After much research, here is a list of terms and how they are used in this series:

"Christmas"—refers to the entire season, not simply one day.

"Christmas time"—Dickens uses this term, but always as two words (not the "Christmastime" we are used to seeing).

"Holyday"—a formal term used to reference specific religious days, including, but not limited to Epiphany, Ash Wednesday, Good Friday, Easter, Whitsunday, and Christmas Day.

"Merry Christmas"—used by Dickens. The term "Happy Christmas" only became popular later.

"Christmas holidays" and "jolly holidays"—though often in England the term "holiday" refers to a break from school and work during the summer, both Dickens and Austen use the term "Christmas holidays" and Dickens even once says "jolly holidays," so I chose to include both terms in this story as well.

"Greetings of the season," "festive season," "the season," and "winter season"—all also show up in Dickens's and Austen's stories.

I hope you find this story memorable and that it brings a bit more light to your jolly holidays!

Merry Christmas and God bless us every one.

To Erin,
Ever the one to bring the hope and light of Christmas year round.

"Are you the Spirit, sir, whose coming was foretold to me?" asked Scrooge.

"I am!"

The voice was soft and gentle. Singularly low, as if instead of being so close beside him, it were at a distance.

"Who, and what are you?" Scrooge demanded.

"I am the Ghost of Christmas Past …
Rise! and walk with me!"

A Christmas Carol
by Charles Dickens

CHAPTER ONE

She was going to ruin everything.

Belle knew she would. Sitting alone in the drawing room, Belle ran a hand over her skirt, smoothing nonexistent wrinkles for the dozenth time. The room held so many memories, yet this Christmas, it somehow felt foreign at the same time. Taking a deep breath—the room smelled of roasting vegetables and old furniture—she tried to still her racing heart.

How long had she anticipated this moment? It had been three years since he'd left, seven years since he'd promised to take her away from all the misery and loneliness that filled her life. But no, she'd been waiting for this moment for longer than that. She'd been waiting since she'd first met him all those years ago—thirteen years, to be exact. Thirteen years, eleven months, and fifteen days.

Her gaze wandered to the tall windows. That day had been snowy, just as this one was. Belle stood and moved slowly toward the windows. She placed a hand against the glass. The chill from outside seeped through her gloves and pricked her fingertips. Thirteen years was a long time to hold out hope. But she'd hold on for another thirteen years if only he would do as he had said he would—if he would marry her and prove she wasn't the forgotten nobody everyone claimed her to be.

Belle caught sight of her reflection in the window glass. Oh, good heavens, she was starting to cry. She blinked several times; she *was* going to ruin everything. She hadn't seen him in years. Their long-awaited reunion shouldn't include puffy eyes and decidedly unromantic sniffles.

The door behind her opened. The light from the hallway beyond reflected in the glass in front of her, a wavy, hazy line of bliss against the dreariness outside. The tall figure of a man moved into the room behind her. He'd come. All these years of waiting, and he was finally home once more.

Belle spun on her heel and flew across the room, her feet outstretching her thoughts.

But the moment her thoughts caught up to her, Belle pulled herself up short. An embarrassing realization sunk in. This wasn't *him* at all. The man was too tall, his jaw too prominent, his hair the wrong shade of brown, and his eyes far too blue.

"Belle?" he asked.

She listed her head; this man was quite familiar, but she couldn't quite recall—

Then he smiled. Oh, Belle knew that smile.

"James," she said enthusiastically, hurrying the rest of the way toward him. No one smiled like he did: one part sincere love of life, one part mischief, and at least three parts curiosity regarding all the world around him.

He took hold of one of her hands in his own, bowing over it.

Belle opened her mouth to say how pleased she was to see him again, but then realized what she'd said only moments ago. "Pardon me," she said quickly. "I suppose I should greet you as Mr. Radcliff now."

"Now? Has something changed since last we met?"

"We are not children as we were then." That glorious festive season the three of them had spent together had been the happiest few weeks of her life.

"Please don't tell me I have to call you *Miss Young* now?"

"Would you be terribly put out?"

"More than you know," he said. He still hadn't let go of her hand, and he gave it a small squeeze. It sent a warm rush up her arm; how she'd missed the kindness and goodwill she'd always found in James.

He glanced around as though expecting someone to be standing beside her. And why wouldn't he? Young ladies did not often attend the dinner parties of unattached bachelors alone. Certainly not *titled* ladies who garnered respect and esteem wherever they went.

Before he could ask, she answered the question she knew must be on his mind. "My aunt and cousin were indisposed tonight." Which meant, of course, that neither her aunt nor her cousin deemed it worth their while to join the small reunion of friends. Ever since Belle's cousin had fallen into good graces with an eligible duke, everyone else fell quite suddenly beneath them. Then again, Belle had always been beneath her aunt and cousin...as well as everyone else. Someday, after she married the man of her dreams, that would change. She would have a title, and with it, the much-wanted approval of her family.

"I was in America for so long," James said, "I half expected to return and find you with a husband and a babe in your arms."

"I am as you see me." Silly man. James couldn't have returned home to find her already wed because *he* had been with James in America this entire time. Three years. Three very long years.

The echo of boots against the floor brought Belle's head around once more.

There, standing in the doorway, was the man she'd been waiting years for.

Fezzi.

Belle's gaze locked with his. She couldn't move.

He was here.

Finally, the wait was over. His grin spread fully across his face, and he moved to her. Good naturedly, he elbowed James out of the way and took not one, but both of Belle's hands in one of his own.

"Yo ho, Belle," he said, his tone full of as much joy as she felt. "It has been too long."

"*Far* too long," she echoed back.

"I'm so very happy you are here." His smile grew yet wider. She had not thought such a thing was possible, yet there it was. "Just wait until you see my surprise."

Surprise? A skittering, joyous awareness pricked across her skin.

Fezzi turned and wrapped a hand tightly against James's arm. "George is here."

The pricking subsided. Belle struggled to keep her brow from falling. Something about the way Fezzi said *George* felt off, out of place amidst their happy reunion. She had no idea who George was, or why the man was important...But wasn't tonight's invitation about seeing one another again? After so many years, when the simple note from his mother, Lady Wilkins, had come, asking her to join them tonight for a family dinner, Belle had thought...

"George?" James repeated. His jaw tightened, and his gaze jumped from Fezzi to Belle and back again.

"Yes." Fezzi was clearly elated. "The whole family, in fact. It took some doing, but I finally convinced Mr. Smith to leave America for a time and travel back with me. Of course, I agreed when he said he would have to bring his family along."

The lightness in James's tone was gone, but the happiness

in Fezzi's only grew. There was something Belle was missing about the whole exchange. She suddenly knew a pointed awareness regarding how much she'd missed these past years—she, being the one left behind, while James and Fezzi had traveled across the ocean.

"Did you meet this Mr. Smith in America?" she asked, wishing she didn't feel quite so naive.

"Yes, just before James had to leave," Fezzi said, letting go of her hands and stepping back. His gaze moved to the door he'd entered through only moments ago. "They'll be here any minute."

"They're coming *here*?" James asked. "Tonight?"

"Of course, old man," Fezzi said, quite as though James had asked something to which he should have known the answer. Fezzi dropped his voice and leaned in toward James. "I spent quite a bit of time over at the Smiths' house after you left." He gave James a knowing smile and then returned to watching the door.

Belle felt as though she was being effectively forced out of the conversation. She placed her hands demurely in front of herself. *Always a lady*. They were the only words she could still remember her mother, who had died when she was young, speaking. *Always a lady*.

Fezzi was quite intent on watching the door, so Belle ventured to reenter the conversation by speaking to James instead. "Were you terribly disappointed in having to return to England before you'd anticipated?" she asked. She'd heard he'd had to come home early because of estate troubles, though from what she'd heard since then, all was set to rights now. Still, it had required he return home before Fezzi, and that could not have been to his liking.

James watched Fezzi closely, while Fezzi seemed to have quite forgotten his two closest friends were standing beside him.

"Yes," James said slowly, not looking over at her. "I had hoped—"

The sounds of several pairs of feet, as well as the echoes of voices, came from the corridor beyond.

"They're here," Fezzi said in an excited whisper. Without looking back at her, he hurried toward the door. The voices drew closer. There was a deep masculine voice, and a heavy female voice, probably an elderly matron. Mr. Smith's wife, perhaps? Though Belle could hear no one else speaking, she could hear what must have been the footfalls of at least four or more people.

James moved up beside her. "Did Fezzi tell you about...George?"

"No," she replied. "He never mentioned the man in any of his letters." Which, granted, had been few and far between. They'd been nearly nonexistent this past year. She'd often fluctuated between worry that he'd forgotten her and determined resoluteness, telling herself that it was unseemly for an unattached gentleman to write a lady with whom he had no understanding. Their secret was their own, after all, and he was only trying to protect her good name; or so she told herself.

Belle glanced up at James. His tight expression did not provide any comfort.

"Come in, come in," Fezzi said, opening the door wider and standing back. A gentleman with gray hair and a black cane in his hand waltzed through the door first, an equally white-haired woman on his arm. "Mr. and Mrs. Smith, you are quite welcome."

The two bowed and curtsied respectively.

"It is a great pleasure to see you again, Lord Wilkins," the woman said to Fezzi.

"Hear, hear," the man at her side agreed. Their voices matched the ones Belle had heard earlier; these were no doubt the two who had spoken.

Two young girls walked in next, probably only barely old enough to be out of the nursery. Both were blonde and wore nearly identical pink dresses, though one was a bit taller, the angles of her face marking her as the older sister.

"May I introduce you all to my dear friends, Mr. Radcliff and Miss Young," Fezzi said. "This is Mr. Charles Smith, his lovely wife, and these are his two youngest daughters, Miss Sarah and Miss Nancy." Both girls curtsied in turn. "And this," Fezzi took the hand of the last individual to walk through the door. She was a lovely woman, probably a year or two younger than Belle. Her hair was set in perfect ringlets, framing a face of delicate pale skin and a perfect button nose.

"This," Fezzi said, his eyes never leaving the young woman's face, "is Miss Georgiana Smith."

CHAPTER TWO

The idiot hadn't told her.

James glanced at Belle, then back at Fezzi. Blast Fezzi and his narrow-minded, amorous ideals. He *hadn't told Belle!* What had the coxcomb been about? James wanted to reach out and take Belle's hand once more. He'd enjoyed the brief touch far more than he ought—she was in love with his best friend and cousin, after all—but he only stepped a bit closer so that her shoulder brushed his arm. He hoped she understood the gesture for what it was—a show of support.

Poor Belle looked suddenly far paler than she had only moments ago.

James nearly growled aloud. How had Fezzi not told Belle about Miss Georgiana Smith? He'd promised James he would write Belle. After that insipid ball, it had been painfully obvious Fezzi was taken with Miss Smith. Only two weeks later, James had been called back to England. While packing, he'd made Fezzi promise him—repeatedly—that should things grow more serious between him and Miss Smith that he would write and let Belle know.

James had never asked Fezzi outright what his intentions

were toward Belle, but after the month the trio had spent together during Christmas time all those years ago, it had been clear to James Belle had set her cap at Fezzi and did so fully expecting her affections to be returned.

"George, dear, you remember Mr. Radcliff. And this is Miss Young," Fezzi said, finishing the introductions.

The woman, whose smile showed just as many teeth as James remembered, glanced between them. "Belle. Well, I'll be." She stepped forward, her eyes staying on Belle. "I must say, I have heard plenty about you."

Belle stiffened beside him. No doubt, she was wishing she could say the same about Miss Smith.

"It is a pleasure to meet you," Belle finally said. She put forth a good show; only someone who knew her well would have heard the tightness about her words. Though perhaps James only flattered himself. They'd spent no more than a month together, and it had been three years previous. It was foolish of him to assume he understood Belle at all. Foolish though it may have been, he felt certain he had not misinterpreted her tone.

Miss Smith reached toward Fezzi, looping an arm through his. "I must admit that I wasn't at all sure about meeting this 'Miss Belle Young' Fezzi always talked about. I hadn't known him a week before I started to wonder if all his talk was an exaggeration. But now I see you're every bit as lovely as he said you were."

It was clear to James that Miss Smith was as prone to chattiness as he remembered. It wasn't that she was unkind; indeed, her compliment to Belle seemed quite sincere. Still, if ever a woman looked in need of a little rescue, it was Belle.

"It truly is very good to see you again." James said the first thing that came to mind, hoping to redirect the conversation away from the woman at his side and give her time to collect herself. "Was your trip across the ocean uneventful?"

"Oh, lands no." Miss Smith readily turned toward him. "Ma was quite sick, and Papa was so busy helping her that I had my hands full with Sarah and Nancy." Her eyes sparked as she glanced behind her. "And *what* a handful they were."

Sarah, the older of the two, stepped forward a bit. "I'm not the one who insisted on curling my hair in papers *every night* on the way over."

Miss Smith patted her curls. "Yes, being beautiful can be such a burden." She laughed, Fezzi joining in.

Miss Smith had a better sense of humor than James remembered, and she lacked any arrogance or self-importance that might make her intolerable. There was no reason for James to dislike the woman, per se. Only, why would Fezzi even glance her way when he had someone like Belle who was clearly waiting for him? The only reason James could come up with was that Fezzi was blind. Or utterly stupid.

Dinner was announced and everyone filed from the room. Fezzi led the way, Miss Smith—"George" as he continued to call her—on his arm, even as he explained that his mother had a headache and would not be joining them as originally planned after all. They were followed by Mr. and Mrs. Smith and then the youngest two Miss Smiths.

Soon, it was only himself and Belle in the room.

She looked quite pale, even as she bit her bottom lip in uncertainty. Cursing Fezzi to the devil yet again, he stretched an elbow out to her.

Without looking his way, Belle placed her hand lightly against his arm. They took one step toward the door, then a second.

"She's quite perfect, isn't she?" Belle said, her voice far weaker than before.

James couldn't, in good conscience, say anything against Miss Smith; it wasn't as though Fezzi's lack of judgment was her fault. Still, if he complimented Miss Smith highly, it would feel like he was deserting to the enemy. "She is a nice enough woman, I suppose." Hopefully that was a good middle-ground statement.

"Is her family well-to-do?"

His brow creased; that hadn't been at all what he'd anticipated her asking. "I believe so. It is my understanding that the Smith family is well respected. The Americans do not have titles as we have here, but I would go so far as to say they are one of the highest esteemed families within their community."

Belle's shoulders dropped slightly. "Then she is not a nobody, then."

Not a nobody? What did that mean?

"James, Belle," Fezzi called from inside the dining room. "Don't tell me you've forgotten your way since last you visited."

They had been walking rather slow. Tucking Belle's hand a little closer to himself, James hurried her forward.

Her soft voice continued to echo about his head. *She is not a nobody, then.*

CHAPTER THREE

"And how was your evening with the handsome Fezzi last night?"

Belle didn't look up from the small bit of fabric in one hand and the needle and thread in the other. Her cousin, Harriet, only called Lord Wilkins "Fezzi" when she was bent on teasing Belle. Fezzi permitted but a few people to call him by the nickname he'd received while at Eton. Belle felt quite proud that she'd been deemed one of them.

Harriet certainly had not.

"It was very nice to see him again," Belle said. At least her voice didn't falter. She'd spent most of the night, after returning home from Easthill Manor, tossing and turning in bed. Fezzi's preference for another woman had been quite clear during dinner.

"Has he not proposed marriage already?" Harriet's tone was high and dripping with fake sympathy. "By the way you've been pining over him these past years, I thought for sure he'd disembark upon arrival and drop to one knee within the week."

Belle had believed so herself once. But that was before the one-year trip had stretched into three, before Fezzi's letters had grown scarce. Still, she wasn't about to admit as much to Harriet.

"Oh." Harriet stuck out her lower lip. "Has he cast you aside? Finally seen enough of the world to think twice about offering for you?"

Her comments hit far too close to the mark. Belle's hands began to shake. She kept her head down—responding to her cousin only ever brought out yet more vitriol—and stuck her needle through the green fabric in her hand.

Harriet leaned back, slouching in a most unladylike manner across the grand settee. "I warned you this day would come."

One of these days, Belle would learn the art of ignoring her cousin. She would let the only slightly veiled insults roll off her. Heaven knew Harriet gave her plenty of opportunities to practice; nonetheless, Belle hadn't yet mastered the skill.

"You have no parents, hardly any dowry, and very little in the way of charm or beauty to recommend you."

The needle slipped, stabbing Belle in the finger. The sting brought tears to her eyes. She pulled her hand back quickly, lest her blood spoil her small creation, and stuck her finger in her mouth.

"Don't get mad at me," Harriet continued. "I only tell you for your own benefit. Any woman ought to know the truth about herself and her prospects."

Belle shook her hand out and blinked away the tears. Against her better judgment, she scowled at Harriet. Belle knew full well that her hair was rather a muddy shade of blonde and it never held a curl properly. Her eyes were an uninteresting blue and her figure dull. Fezzi had never overly cared for such things, so Belle hadn't worried. America had changed him in more ways than one.

"Miss Young," Aunt Agnes's voice snapped from behind Belle. "What is wrong with your hand?"

Harriet sat up straight and answered for her. "She was being clumsy again and poked herself with her silly little needle."

Belle pressed her lips tightly together.

Aunt Agnes shook her head as she crossed the drawing room and sat on the settee beside her daughter. "I don't see why you are so bent on making yet more of those *things*." Her lips curled as she said the word.

"They're puppets," Belle said softly. "For the Twelfth Night children's performance."

Aunt Agnes only shook her head, then turned and faced Harriet. "You will never believe what has happened," Aunt Agnes said, excitement filling her tone. "We are *not* to join the Brisbanes this year for Christmas time after all."

Belle's head came up quickly, though neither looked at her or took notice.

"We're not?" Harriet asked, sounding quite distraught.

Belle felt the same. Suppose her aunt and cousin decided to stay *here*, at Wilmington Bury? She slowly lowered her puppet, not half done, into her lap. Suppose they actually joined her next time Lady Wilkins invited her over? Suppose they made themselves known at every Christmas time festival and traditional gathering she fully expected to spend with Fezzi?

Aunt Agnes only lifted her chin higher. "Oh no, we will be keeping company with a certain gentleman of much higher standing than the Brisbanes."

A small bit of calm reentered Belle's chest, even as Harriet's eyes grew wide.

Aunt Agnes held out a small letter. "First, you must thank your dear Mama for securing us such elevated society this Christmas."

Harriet wasn't so patient. "Tell me who it is." Her hands flew to her mouth. "It isn't...Don't tell me...Is it really?"

"Yes, dearest," Aunt Agnes said. "We will be staying with his lordship, the Duke of Pembroke."

Harriet squealed.

Belle relaxed. How, exactly, Aunt Agnes ever secured them an invitation to stay at Stonewell Castle with the Silent Duke, as he was called, Belle could not fathom. However, neither did she care. Her own Christmas holidays were safe. Her time with Fezzi was her own again—well, as much her own as it could be with Miss Smith staying at Easthill Manor. Belle tried yet again to shake the image of the beautiful woman on Fezzi's arm out of her head as her aunt and cousin's voices filled the room around her.

"I am sorry, Belle," Aunt Agnes said. "The invitation did not specifically mention you and I don't feel we could trespass on his lordship's good nature quite so far as to bring you uninvited."

Belle did her best to appear slightly disappointed yet accepting—she always worried that if her two last remaining relatives ever found out how much she looked forward to being left behind during Christmas time, they might choose to stay just to spite her. "I quite understand."

"Oh, Mama," Harriet said, her voice almost a wail, "I must have new dresses. And a new spencer. And a new bonnet and new boots—"

"Yes, yes, you certainly must. We will see to it at once."

Belle slowly picked up her small bits of cloth and thread and silently made her way to the door. Her aunt and cousin were so wrapped up in planning a snare for the infamous Silent Duke that they didn't even notice her slip out of the room. Belle paused just outside the door. Aunt Agnes's deep alto voice mingled with Harriet's shrill soprano. Belle didn't begrudge her cousin joy at being invited to stay with a duke. She would be elated if ever such an opportunity fell in her lap.

But it was like Harriet had said. Belle was an orphan of a

father who held no title and left her no dowry. She would never receive such an invitation. Not yet, anyway.

Slowly, she turned toward the stairs. The night had settled in unusually early, yet she could easily find her way in the dark. As she stepped up the stairs, she pulled her shoulders back, lifted her chin, and allowed her mind to float to its favorite spot.

Someday, she would no longer be *Miss Young*; she would be *Lady* Wilkins, a countess and a person of high standing among society. La, but the people who would beg to be introduced to her. And the dresses she'd own! She'd see to it that her abigail learned how to style her hair in the most current fashion and she'd never be forced to wear another's discarded pearls out in company.

Belle reached the landing but didn't drop her air of importance. She would be invited to all the best parties. Ha! Imagine. She might be invited by His Grace more often than either Aunt Agnes *or* Harriet. Wouldn't that be scrumptious? She could see it now—

Another invitation from his lordship? Why, I only returned home from there three months ago. Truly, His Grace must learn to host a party without me. Fezzi is growing quite jealous as it is.

Fezzi. Her chin dropped at the thought of him; her next step was not nearly so regal.

He and Miss Smith *were* only good friends, weren't they? The tightness in her stomach told her otherwise.

Belle reached her door and slowly turned the knob. How well she could remember the day she first met Fezzi. For years, ever since her parents had died, Belle's aunt and cousin had left her behind at Christmas time. Some years they went to London, others to see the Brisbanes. But no matter where they went, they always found an excuse to leave Belle behind.

They said she was too young—despite only being nine months Harriet's junior.

They said she was too sick—despite having no cough, fever, or sniffles.

They said she was too quiet by nature and surely would not enjoy herself spending Christmas among company she'd never met. They never seemed to realize, or care, that the only reason she'd never met the Brisbanes, or anyone else, was because they always left her at home.

Those first several years were miserable. Wilmington Bury was barren with no one to hang holly or evergreen boughs. There was no music, except for the little she played herself. There were no presents, no cheery wishes of a 'Merry Christmas,' nothing that had filled the season her first six years of life.

Belle picked up a candle, barely more than a stub now, and lit it from the small embers in the hearth. Then, one year, Lady Wilkins had heard of the little girl left behind at Christmas time. How Lady Wilkins had first learned of Belle's predicament she still hadn't pieced together. Perhaps the preacher had told her? Or one of their other neighbors?

Either way, Lady Wilkins had insisted Belle join their family, claiming that Belle would be a good companion for her daughter, Fezzi's sister, Eliza. It didn't matter that Eliza was five years Belle's senior; the entire family made Belle feel like one of their own. They invited her to every festivity, every year, after that.

Though she and Eliza always got on well, it was Fezzi who had truly made her feel welcome. As children, he'd sneak her lemon tarts from the kitchen or take her hand and pull her behind him whenever they were targets of snowball fights. They grew, and he would sing carols as she played the pianoforte or slip her the winning raisin when they played snapdragon.

Slowly, Belle sank into the chair nearest the fire. The year before Fezzi left for America, he'd pulled her aside on Twelfth

Night and promised her—most ardently—that when he came back, he'd see to taking her away from all the misery at Wilmington Bury.

Belle picked up the puppet—a man in a green riding cloak. She had to squint to avoid sticking herself with the needle once more. Fezzi had never said "marriage" specifically, yet at the time, she'd felt quite certain that's what he'd meant.

Once she married Fezzi, once she was *Lady* Wilkins, her whole world would change. She was certain of it. She would be *wanted* at winter balls. The *ton* would esteem her as acceptable. Her aunt and cousin would no longer be ashamed of her.

But the way Fezzi had watched Miss Smith last night...the way he'd laughed at her witty comments and agreed with her on everything. Belle lowered the puppet, too distracted to focus. Had she been mistaken in Fezzi's regard? Or had his meeting Miss Smith changed things between them?

James had admitted that Miss Smith wasn't a *nobody* like Belle herself was. It very well could be, now that Fezzi had seen the world, that he'd realized marrying her would be nothing short of settling. It was just as Harriet had told Belle so many times before; Fezzi could do far better.

Belle worried over her bottom lip—perhaps the only unladylike habit Aunt Agnes had never fully chastised out of her. If Fezzi chose to marry another, what would she do? She knew no one else, and her aunt had already made it clear she wasn't going to waste any time or money on a London Season for Belle.

Suppose she *never* married? Suppose Harriet wed and left Belle alone with Aunt Agnes? Belle would be seen as nothing more than a lady's companion, forever at Aunt Agnes's side, doing all she was commanded. Fetching drinks. Grabbing a shawl. Moving a chair closer to the light.

Belle slowly stroked the puppet in her lap. Eventually, Aunt Agnes would force Belle to give up the few things she did which brought her happiness, such as the puppet show she did each year for the children of the servants and tenants. Aunt Agnes had always frowned on the tradition, but she was never around during Christmas time and so had allowed it.

But that would change if Harriet married and moved away and left Belle behind.

Belle stood; sewing was quite impossible in her frame of mind. Her stomach was all aflutter. She quickly returned the puppet to the small chest at the foot of her bed where the others were—some completed, most not. Belle shut it, then took to pacing the chilly room.

She couldn't tolerate such a life. Heaven help her—perhaps she was being selfish—but she just couldn't tolerate it. Fezzi was her only hope. Her only chance at a life away from Wilmington Bury.

Turning toward the small fire, she set her jaw. No matter what, and despite Miss Smith's unexpected arrival, Belle was not going to roll over and give up on her single opportunity to be happy in life.

Fezzi *had* promised her.

The hope she felt whenever she thought back to that Christmas was all that had kept her going many times these past three years.

She would hold on to that hope now. She wouldn't meekly be pushed into the shadows again. She needed a way out of this house—a way to escape her aunt and cousin. If it took a bit of determination on her part then so be it.

CHAPTER FOUR

"Hurry in, dear, and shut the carriage door," Lady Wilkins called out the moment a footman opened it for Belle. "I must say, it is a very brisk day."

Belle did as she was told and sat directly beside Lady Wilkins. The carriage was far warmer inside than the wind was outside. Probably the blessings of a well-warmed brick or two.

"Do we have much to see to today?" Belle asked the older woman even while situating her skirts more tightly around her legs. Though the space was warm, the brief walk from Wilmington Bury's front door to the carriage had drawn out gooseskin along her arms and legs.

"Not terribly much," Lady Wilkins replied.

The carriage lurched forward. The regular sound of wood creaking mingled with the light crunch of wheels rolling over snow. "I vowed I would not make the same mistake I did last year and wait until mid-December before ordering breads and the like for our Christmas boxes. We will see to that first. Then, I was hoping to grab a few items for Eliza's sweet little one."

Though the curtains were drawn around the windows, Belle knew the moment they'd crossed through the towering gate and left Wilmington Bury behind. She silently relaxed; Harriet had been bustling about the house all morning, unable to speak about anything other than her upcoming trip.

"I am glad Eliza and her little girl are doing so well," Belle said. "But I am sad they won't be joining us this year." She and Eliza had begun to grow apart these past few years, but Belle still would have been happy to see her friend again.

"Yes, you and me both," Lady Wilkins said with a sad sigh.

Their ride together carried on in such a manner. Talk of babies and Westminster was followed by fashion and yule logs. Was it any wonder Belle looked forward to this time all the year long? With Lady Wilkins often in London during the spring and summer, they had much to catch up on whenever the snows began.

They turned down the busiest street in all of Dunwell. Which, granted, wasn't saying much. Their little town was not a large one, despite sitting quite close to the River Tyne. The carriage rolled to a stop and a footman had the door open immediately.

The sweet smell of freshly baked bread wafted into the carriage. Belle stepped out. The cold air bit against her nose and cheeks. Blessedly, her ears were tucked beneath the brim of her bonnet; despite it being rather plain, it did keep her warmer.

"I shall need several dozen loaves of bread," Lady Wilkins said, stepping out behind her. "Though I don't care to be overly particular this year. Perhaps I'm growing old, but I'd rather let the baker choose how many of this variety of bread or that."

Belle nodded her understanding. The rows of shops towered above her, fading away in the winter fog around them. Was it just her, or was the air more invigorating when not underneath the shadow of Wilmington Bury?

"Are you coming, dear?"

Belle turned to find Lady Wilkins standing in the bakery doorway, the warm firelight from the shop framing her wrinkled smile.

"No," Belle said, taking another deep breath of winter air. "I think I'll just enjoy the fresh air. You go ahead."

"The fresh air? My dear, it's well below freezing."

"You said yourself you won't be long, and I promise to step inside if I grow at all uncomfortable."

Lady Wilkins shook her head. "As you wish." She stepped inside fully, the door swinging shut with a soft whine.

Belle turned and faced the road. Not many people were out, and the few who were kept their hats down or their bonnets tight against their faces. She may have known a few of the people around her, but with everyone so bundled up, she couldn't be certain. Either way, she was simply grateful to be away from home and out in the brisk air.

With her next breath, the cold tingled inside her lungs, then billowed out around her mouth. Winter had long been her favorite time of year. The horse hitched to Lady Wilkins's carriage tossed its mane. The poor beast probably wasn't enjoying the cold as much as Belle was. Then again, he had to return to an equally cold barn with no warm hearths and no friendly smiles. With Aunt Agnes and Cousin Harriet leaving the next morning, Belle was fully looking forward to removing herself to Easthill Manor, as she did every year once they'd left, and enjoying the remainder of the festive season.

Belle closed her eyes and tipped her head back. Soon, instead of slipping out unnoticed to spend the darkest hours alone in her room with only the smallest of candles, she would be welcomed in the drawing room late into the night. Instead of being talked down to and reminded of how very plain her appearance was, she would be included in discussions on happenings of the neighborhood and the happy addition in Eliza's life.

"Miss Young?"

Belle opened her own eyes to find a very young pair looking up at her. The girl could not have been twelve, and her tattered clothing hung more like a sack than a dress.

Belle stooped down, coming to eye level with the girl. "Yes, I am Miss Young. What is your name?"

The girl glanced either direction, a smile brightening her face. "Lily, miss. My uncle's a footman in Lady Wilkins's house."

The little girl's cheerful expression touched Belle's heart. "A footman? Then I'd wager you help him get the door for all the finest ladies and gentlemen."

The little girl giggled. "I'm too short."

"But you would look most distinguished."

Another snicker, then Lily glanced over her shoulder once more. This time, Belle saw a man standing across the road watching their interaction.

"Uncle said I'm not to bother you," Lily continued. "Only, I did so want to ask, will you be doing another puppet show on Twelfth Night?"

A small blossom of happiness spread within Belle. Her puppet shows were such a silly thing—especially according to Aunt Agnes. It wasn't as though the show put food in anyone's stomachs or warmer blankets on their beds. Truly, it wasn't anything noble or meaningful. But Belle did enjoy it, and she liked to think the young children of servants and tenants enjoyed it too.

"Would you like another puppet show this year?" Belle put on a pretense of considering the notion.

"Oh yes, miss," Lily declared. "I loved it when the hunter rescued the princess."

"You don't say," another far deeper voice said from just behind Belle. "Because that just so happened to be my favorite part as well."

Belle stood, turning, and found James beside her. "How long have you been standing there?"

Instead of answering, he only lifted an eyebrow and smiled all the broader.

"Please," Lily said again. Clearly the young girl was not to be distracted. "We all want another puppet show."

"You have convinced me," Belle said dramatically. "I shall have to put another one on this year just for you."

Lily cried out in joy, then spun around and rushed off to the man who'd been watching them silently. He scooped Lily up the moment she got to him, then bowed Belle's direction before turning and disappearing into the fog.

"I'm glad you're to put on another show," James said. "I quite enjoyed the one you did a few years ago."

"I'm surprised you remember it at all." He'd only been at Easthill Manor the one Christmas time, and that had been three years ago.

"Remember it? I found it quite..." James seemed to search for the right word.

Belle felt a bit of the joy she'd been sharing with Lily ebb away. "Silly?" she offered. "Pointless? Beneath one of our station?" Those were all things Aunt Agnes had said many a time. Fezzi, too, then and again.

James's brow creased. "No. I was going to say diverting, but that didn't fit. I think the word I'm looking for is somewhere closer to imaginative, or even impressive."

His estimation surprised her. "So you don't think my puppet shows are nonsense?" She tried to affect an uncaring air, but her tone made plain her serious desire to know.

"Not in the least," he said, wholly sincere.

Belle ducked her head, allowing her bonnet to hide her smile. His praise meant more to her than he could possibly know. "They do take a great deal of time to piece together."

"The puppets I saw three years ago were quite exquisite; I

rather wonder that you don't use up all the thread in Dunwell every year stitching in all those fine details."

"You have no idea how true that statement is, for I am forever snapping the thread while working." She laughed softly at herself. Of course, it didn't help that she often worked at night, when firelight was the only lighting available. "I'm quite nearly out of every color. But enough of that. What brings you into town on this fine day?"

"Ah." His voice turned stilted and he rocked back slightly. He slipped a hand beneath the thick fabric of his overcoat and pulled out a bit of paper. "A letter from my man of business."

"Nothing troublesome, I hope?"

"No—" He drew the word out like he wasn't fully convinced of it himself. "Well," he finally amended, "nothing *too* troublesome."

"At this time of year, that is most unfortunate." Christmas time should be a season of joy and plenty, with no troubles in sight. Belle knew it could not always be so, but she still wished for it. "If there is anything I can do to help, you will tell me?" The moment the words left her mouth, Belle wished them back. What kind of arrogant nonsense made her think she could help James with his estate? "Forgive me." She curtsied lightly. "I don't know why I said that."

"Because you are a kind woman and a good friend," James replied without hesitation.

Belle's cheeks warmed despite the frigid air around her. In fact, her face was probably quite red from all his flattery. Why did she react so? It was only James, after all. Though Belle had little practice with flattery of any sort, from any source.

She shook her head. "Even if that were the case, matters of an estate are certainly beyond me." Running an estate probably required quite a bit of mathematical knowledge and an understanding of farms and tenants and leases.

James listed his head. "What makes you say that?"

What did he mean, what made her say that? "A lady is not brought up to such things."

His hand took hold of hers. The touch was unexpected, but certainly not unpleasant. Quite the opposite, in fact. She found her hand in his to be very comforting, even taking into account the small flutterings it set off in her stomach.

"Belle," he said, his voice rich and deep. "I don't think you give yourself enough credit."

The door to the bakery swung open and Lady Wilkins stepped out. "James, good day to you."

She stepped up beside Belle, and Belle pulled her hand away from James. No doubt Lady Wilkins had seen the brief moment of tenderness. What would she think? Though Belle had never spoken of Fezzi's promise to her with his mother, she doubted the woman was blind to Belle's hopes. And now, she was holding the hand of another man?

Still, when Lady Wilkins spoke, she seemed not the least bit put out or even surprised. "Belle and I had not anticipated running into you today."

"Business brought me into town shortly after you left," James explained.

"Where is your horse?" Lady Wilkins asked.

What a fool Belle had been; she'd not even thought to ask such a thing. Instead, she'd prattled on about puppets and other absurdities. Belle glanced around but saw no horse tied up nearby.

"I walked, my lady," James said. "It is such a nice winter day, and Easthill Manor is not so terribly far."

Lady Wilkins shook her head. "You sound just like Belle. Frankly, I cannot understand the sentiment. I'm quite content being driven about in my warm carriage." She stepped between them, heading for the conveyance. A footman hurried over, opening the door. "Now, if you will excuse us, Belle and I have several other things to see to before returning home."

"Yes, of course," James said.

Belle followed the unspoken direction and moved up to the carriage as well. Lifting her skirt with one hand, she made to step inside. James's hand found hers again, and he helped her up.

As Belle sat beside Lady Wilkins, James held on to her for a moment longer than necessary. Despite the gloves they both wore, she did enjoy the feeling until he let go and stepped away.

She leaned back against the squabs, her mind replaying James's words. *You do not give yourself enough credit.*

The footman closed the door, and all too soon the carriage rolled through town even as the memory of James's smile and encouraging words brought one last blush to Belle's cheeks.

CHAPTER FIVE

James watched as the carriage rolled away. He'd not expected to see Belle and Lady Wilkins any more than it seemed they had expected to see him. Nonetheless, he wasn't the least bit put out by the small delay to his meeting.

The carriage turned a corner, but James stood on, watching the fog swirl around him and the surrounding buildings. The unanticipated bright spot of his morning, Belle's sweet conversation with the niece of a footman, was over now. He could only get on with the difficult task at hand.

He pulled the letter from his coat pocket and opened it. The address directed him to a small building not far from the bakery. Walking down the street, his mind stayed on Belle and how pleasant it had been to run into her.

Did she realize how often she chewed on her bottom lip? He'd seen her do it many times three years ago when they'd both holidayed at Easthill Manor. He'd somehow figured she'd likely grown out of the habit in adulthood, the way it was always accompanied by an innocent expression of worry and uncertainty. It was rather endearing that she had not.

James checked the numbers atop the doors as he passed. Just a couple more. No doubt Belle was aware of her own habit, but did she know just *how often* she did it? He'd counted twice in their brief exchange just now.

James paused. An old wooden door with an equally old and uncared for metal doorknocker rested beneath the number he was searching for.

What he wouldn't give to avoid this meeting today. However, to run and ignore the issue now would leave a metaphoric door open to very real disaster. With a heavy hand, James lifted the knocker and let it clank against the metal plate. He stepped back slightly and waited for it to be opened to him. It was times like this he was tempted to do as Belle so often did and chew his own bottom lip. He knew very little regarding the man on whom he was calling—only that as a moneylender, he knew nearly every man in the surrounding area.

James needed answers regarding one man in particular, and he needed them before anyone else learned the truth.

The door groaned loudly as it swung open. A heavily wrinkled man with a low stoop smiled up at him, the hand holding the door open shaking with age.

"Mr. Scrooge?" James inquired.

The old man laughed. "Not by half." He took a small step back, then another, ever so slowly pulling the door open. "I am Mr. Cratchit. But Mr. Scrooge is..." The man breathed for a minute, then continued once the door was swung open fully. "Mr. Scrooge is in the back. Who shall I say is calling?"

James extended his card.

Mr. Cratchit took it with a small bow. "Very well; wait here, please."

James nodded his understanding and the old man hobbled down the long hallway before them. The space was quite dark; only two small candles lit the hall. The man moved into the shadows at the back of the hall and disappeared. The wind outside wailed, and cold bit against James's back. He turned slightly. Good gracious, the door was pocked with slits and small openings the full length of the wood. It had to cost a fortune to keep such a drafty place warm during the winter.

James tossed his shoulders, shifting his greatcoat better around him. Now that he thought about it, it was hardly any warmer inside the man of business's office than it had been outside. Mr. Scrooge was purported to charge high interest rates to those unlucky enough to need a loan, and this is how he kept his office?

"I see you did not receive my letter," a voice from the shadows said. James could not see the speaker, but it was clearly a man, and one much younger than the elderly gentleman who'd left him minutes ago.

"Actually, I did, sir. That is, if I have the pleasure of addressing Mr. Scrooge."

The man stepped out into the mottled candlelight. "I am he. Though it is of little pleasure to me, and I sincerely doubt it is any better for you." The man was neither particularly old nor young—early forties, most likely. He stood broad of shoulder but was draped in what could not be dismissed as anything finer than last decade's jacket. His hair ran down either side of his face in tight curls, several of which sported as much silver as they did brown. Mr. Scrooge moved closer to James; though the man's face did not appear aged, there were lines about his eyes, the kind one only got from excessive scowling.

"If you received my letter, then why are you come?" Mr. Scrooge said. "I've already expressed to you that I do not know this Mr. Thrup you seek."

"I understand that, sir, but I was hoping some memory of the past may have resurfaced, anything that might point me toward the direction in which he might be found."

Mr. Scrooge muttered something under his breath and

motioned for them both to adjourn into the small room to James's right.

James shifted uncomfortably from one foot to the next before taking the chair Mr. Scrooge offered him. The space was cold and musty; the less time he spent here, the better. Nonetheless, James could not leave until he had some lead on the whereabouts of Mr. Thrup.

"This is of the highest importance, I assure you," he said.

"So you've assured me already." Mr. Scrooge sat behind a large desk.

James chose to ignore the man's gruff demeanor. "I have it on good authority that Mr. Thrup lived in Dunwell some twenty-nine years ago. Might you, perchance, have records of him, at the very least?"

"From nearly three decades ago?" Mr. Scrooge shook his head.

"Perhaps," Mr. Cratchit called out from where he sat at a much smaller desk behind them, "Mr. Jacob once loaned to the man? I am happy to retrieve his records from that year."

James tried to hide his sigh of relief; apparently there *were* records from the year Fezzi was born. He'd heard Mr. Scrooge was a stickler for details and accounts. He'd hoped that tendency was a longstanding one.

Scrooge's scowl only deepened as his gaze moved to his clerk. James could have sworn he saw lines etching yet deeper wrinkles into the man's brow. "Not another word, Bob Cratchit."

The elderly man returned to his own accounts, studious and silent.

"If there are records," James said, "I ask they be searched."

"Why?"

The tension along James's back grew all the tighter. He placed an ankle up against a knee. The chair he'd been offered was naught but solid wood of a very dull variety. Was this all a distinguished man such as Mr. Scrooge supplied for his clients to sit upon? James shifted again, wishing for something which made him feel more like a grown man with wisdom, instead of a schoolboy about to be sent down for the term.

"It must be related to an inheritance," Mr. Scrooge surmised.

James stilled, his jaw clamping tight.

Mr. Scrooge continued, apparently not needing James to admit as much out loud. "What else would drive a young man to such lengths if not money?"

This may have been about his cousin's inheritance—and yes, even about blunt, as heartless as it sounded—but James would not be distracted from his purpose. "You loan money to nearly every working man in Dunwell and beyond. You have for decades. You are my best chance at finding Mr. Thrup and find him, I must."

Mr. Scrooge placed his arms atop his old desk and leaned forward. "Tell me why it is so important, and I will see what my old business partner may have written about the man."

James's stomach rolled. He hadn't told a solitary soul what Mrs. Gaight had confided in him just before she'd passed. Gads, but he was loath to do so now. Still, if he didn't, Mr. Scrooge appeared most determined to turn him away.

He had to find this Mr. Thrup—had to find the man before he made himself known to Fezzi or Lady Wilkins.

"My estate is small and carries no title. I came by it through my mother, strangely enough. A few years ago, I fell on hard times and I had to reduce. I let most of the staff go. However, I kept on an elderly lady by the name of Mrs. Gaight."

"Only the pertinent details, if you please."

James's jaw tightened once again. He blew out a slow breath through his nose. "Very well. Mrs. Gaight grew quite ill last winter. Just before passing, she told me that..." Lud, James could hardly get the words out. Mr. Scrooge watched him closely, and James suddenly became aware that Mr. Cratchit's pen no longer scratched against paper behind him. He hoped telling the two men wouldn't prove a monumental mistake. "She told me that the current Lord Wilkins is..." He couldn't make the word come out.

"Illegitimate," Mr. Scrooge finished for him.

Blast, but that sounded harsh. All James could do was nod.

"And Mr. Thrup is the earl's true father?"

James nodded again. Fezzi was his cousin. Even more so, Fezzi was his best friend. They'd been inseparable while at Eton. James had even convinced his father to let him spend Christmas one year with Fezzi at Easthill Manor. They'd traversed the ocean together. They'd seen America together.

A gentleman did not simply steal his best friend's inheritance out from under him, no matter being in the right.

"What proof did Mrs. Gaight have that convinced you she was telling the truth?"

There hadn't been much. Nonetheless, from the moment James first listened to the aged woman's tale, he hadn't slept well, hadn't been able to sit for long.

"She knew the man's name." James couldn't bring himself to say *Fezzi's father's name*. "She said that while the late Lord Wilkins and his wife appeared most happy on their wedding day"—hang him, but this felt like betraying family—"it must have been for show. Lord Wilkins was gone much, seeing to matters in Parliament, when suddenly it became clear Lady Wilkins was in the family way." James pushed the rest of the words out—the sooner this whole ordeal was over, the better. He was only doing this for Fezzi, after all. He was only doing this to be sure no one took Easthill Manor away from his cousin. "The late Lord Wilkins was sent for and returned just before Lady Wilkins entered her confinement. Mrs. Gaight was quite convinced that he was both surprised and none too pleased to learn of his wife's condition. She told me there was a letter. The late Lord Wilkins had given it to her to destroy, but she'd kept it instead."

James had not been happy to hear she'd kept something so condemning. Yet, she'd said she had no idea, when Fezzi was still a baby, if he would turn out gentle like the late Lord Wilkins, or wild like Mr. Thrup. He could hear Mrs. Gaight's weak and broken voice clearly, as though she was speaking to him now. She claimed she'd kept the letter as proof if ever Fezzi needed to be removed from his position as earl. Grabbing his arm in her trembling hand, Mrs. Gaight had begged James's forgiveness, begged him to clear her conscience.

"And why," Mr. Scrooge asked, "would the late Lord Wilkins have given this letter to a woman who was employed at your estate?"

James pulled himself back to the present. "She was working as Lady Wilkins's lady's maid at the time. Some years ago, however, Mrs. Gaight grew too feeble to hold such a taxing position and I agreed to let her come work for me since my household is decidedly less demanding." And Mrs. Gaight, for some reason, had reminded him of his own mother.

"Huh," Mr. Scrooge grunted as he steepled his fingers. "A name and letter. It's unsubstantial at best."

It was. Yet at the same time, there was just enough of a something to worry James.

"Especially," Mr. Scrooge continued, "considering how many years ago the supposed scandal took place."

Supposed scandal. James could get behind that term. Nothing was certain, and he preferred to think of it that way. Lady Wilkins had always been kind and welcoming toward him. She'd been even more so immediately after his own mother had passed, almost a decade ago.

"All the same, if the right evidence was found, the current

Lord Wilkins could find himself in very hot water," Mr. Scrooge said, sitting back once more.

The more James spoke of the issue, the more he realized he'd been right to treat this as serious from the beginning. "That's why I've come to you. I need to find Mr. Thrup."

"And what will you do once you have found the man?"

"I will see to it that he keeps the truth to himself."

"I suppose you are also searching for the rumored letter. What will you do once you find *it*?"

"Watch it burn."

Mrs. Gaight had claimed she'd left the letter at Easthill Manor when she'd come to work for him. Finding it was the main reason he'd asked Fezzi to let him join them for the Christmas holidays. Finding the letter was imperative.

"Foolish notion," Mr. Scrooge grumbled.

James placed both feet firmly on the ground and leaned forward. "I beg your pardon."

"Your cousin is illegitimate."

There was that word again. It rubbed and scratched against him.

Mr. Scrooge continued on in James's silence. "If he was born out of wedlock, then his father had no true heir. The inheritance would have fallen to his brother next down, who would have passed it on to his oldest son—you. Instead of *Mr. Radcliff*, you should have been, and still could be, *Lord Wilkins*."

James held Mr. Scrooge's gaze without blinking. "He is my cousin and best friend. I'll not take away the home he was raised in, the one he fully expects will always be his own."

"I looked into you when you first contacted me. Your estate is turning only a small profit. You barely have the means to marry or have a family."

Belle's smile came to mind. If James hadn't missed the mark, Fezzi would be doing just that soon enough; provided he come to his senses and ceased allowing Miss Smith to distract him, he would be married directly and soon starting a family. James had always supposed such would be part of his own future, but since returning home after hearing his estate was on the brink of bankruptcy, nothing had been certain.

"What makes you believe I want such a thing?" he asked, trying to hide just how much he truly *did* want it.

"Most idiots do," Mr. Scrooge said, sotto voce, as he stood and moved out from behind the large desk. "With the Wilkins title and estate, you'd be free of monetary troubles the rest of your life."

Didn't he know it. Still, James shook his head, while shifting around to better face Mr. Scrooge. "I don't want to be earl. I just want to know Fezzi is protected."

Mr. Scrooge crossed to a large cabinet and pulled a drawer open. The scraping sound it made put James in mind of the front door of this dark place—moaning and groaning and generally dying from lack of care.

"This is the even-handed dealing of the world," Mr. Scrooge said, his back to James as he rifled through files. "There is nothing on which it is so hard as poverty, and there is nothing it professes to condemn with such severity as the pursuit of wealth!"

As a man who'd been scoffed at more than once for his undeniable lack of title and fortune, James could only sympathize with the man's statement, bitter though it was. "It is an illogical society, to be sure."

Mr. Scrooge pulled out a file with a snort. "Illogical, indeed." He perched a pair of small spectacles atop the end of his nose and flipped the file open. Silently, Mr. Scrooge read.

James didn't want to interrupt the man's perusal of what he hoped were Mr. Jacob's old records and so sat quietly. Soon, though, his fingers began to rap against his thigh. Suppose Mr. Jacob had never had cause to loan to Mr. Thrup? Where would James ever search next? The man had stayed silent this long, though; what were the chances he would make his parentage known now? What would Lady Wilkins do if he tried? Without the late Lord Wilkins still alive and able to defend his wife, James wasn't at all sure. The thought that kept needling James was that Mr. Thrup may just be waiting for Fezzi to wed. Once Fezzi had a family to protect, Mr. Thrup could far more easily demand payment to keep silent.

More than once these past several days, James had been bent on taking Fezzi aside and demanding to know what his intentions were—toward both Belle and Miss Smith. But suppose such an intervention pushed Fezzi toward proposing and marriage was, in fact, just what Mr. Thrup was waiting for?

No, James needed to remain silent on this point for a little while longer. At least until he could locate Mr. Thrup. The letter was also important, but at least he didn't have to worry that it would stroll out of hiding all on its own, announce its horrid secret to Fezzi, and ruin his cousin's life.

Of course, if someone *else* found it—say, while the house was being prepared for a bride—everything could fall apart so very quickly.

Perhaps he should confront Lady Wilkins. The very thought left him feeling sick.

Should he just tell Fezzi?

No. He dismissed that idea immediately. Fezzi would be destroyed by the knowledge.

Devil take it. This whole blasted thing had him spinning around in circles. Every option, every unfounded thought seemed both absurd and reasonable at the same time.

"It appears," Mr. Scrooge finally said, his words dragged out as he was clearly still reading, "my late partner did, in fact, loan a small amount to a man by the name of Mr. Thrup. It was repaid in a timely manner, however, and there appears to be no more on the man."

Great. Now James had yet more proof that he was right to worry since Mr. Thrup did, indeed, exist. But he still had no better idea where to find him.

"Is there no address among the record?" James pressed.

"Mr. Jacob may have departed seven years ago," Mr. Scrooge said, slipping the file back in the large, grime-covered cabinet, "seven years ago this very winter—but we were partners for over half my life. I'd know if there was more information to be had."

James felt his hope sink. So much for finding Mr. Thrup before the man appeared and either ruined Fezzi or demanded blunt to keep quiet.

No matter how desolate it was to admit it, there seemed to be nothing else to learn here. James pushed against the hard chair and stood. "I thank you for your time, sir. And I trust," he added most sternly, "that I can count on your silence in this matter."

Mr. Scrooge shut up the cabinet once more. "I am no gossipy hag. You may be sure. Mr. Cratchit will show you to the door."

It hardly seemed necessary to drag the elderly man away from his desk just to walk beside James for all of ten paces. Still, he felt it best not to argue. He bid Mr. Scrooge a good day, but before he'd gone far, Mr. Scrooge called after him. "And don't throw out the thought of claiming your right as heir just now either. The world is a cruel place. It's every man for himself."

James paused as Mr. Cratchit slowly opened the door for him and turned back toward Mr. Scrooge. "I'd like to think there's a bit more hope for the lot of us than all that."

Mr. Scrooge harrumphed. "Humbug."

James replaced his hat atop his head and took a step outside. Though still cold outside, it was still better than inside that horrid place. It was time James left the grouch to his own dark and cold room.

"Pardon me, sir," Mr. Cratchit said in a low voice.

James turned back around.

"I think...that is to say, sir, that you shouldn't give up on Mr. Jacob. He may yet be able to help us."

James couldn't see how. "Are you proposing we hope for a ghostly visit from the grave?"

Mr. Cratchit smiled, his aged face wrinkling. While Mr. Scrooge's face was etched with years of scowling, it immediately became clear that Mr. Cratchit's was etched with years of smiles. "Mr. Scrooge likes to talk like his previous partner has died, but the truth is he's quite alive and well."

Everything inside James leapt at the news; his chances of finding Mr. Thrup were not over just yet.

"Leave it to me," Mr. Cratchit said. "I think I can convince Mr. Scrooge to provide an introduction."

"That would be most appreciated." James felt like his whole body was suddenly more awake. There was still a chance to protect Fezzi. "Most appreciated, indeed."

Mr. Cratchit nodded and then slipped back inside, closing the door.

James turned back toward the street. He'd been so sure Mr. Thrup would remain untraceable, but now he had reason to hope again. Taking long strides, James turned himself toward Easthill Manor, shaking off the dampness and unpleasantness of the meeting. What a wretched business this all was.

At least he'd heard of it before anyone else had, before Mr. Thrup had chosen to make himself known, and before the letter Mrs. Gaight had kept was accidentally found.

Speaking of the letter, he was determined to find it himself. Find it and burn it. If it took him every waking moment of the Christmas holidays to see to Fezzi's future, then that was what he would do.

CHAPTER SIX

The day had arrived.

Belle stepped out of the carriage—one Fezzi had graciously sent for her—and onto the stone walk in front of Easthill Manor. She'd visited a few times already this winter for dinner parties and the like. She'd even gone into town with Lady Wilkins three times to help the sweet matron ready boxes for the day after Christmas.

But none of those moments compared to this one.

This was the moment she left Wilmington Bury behind, not to return until after Twelfth Night. She breathed in deeply while footmen unloaded her portmanteau and small trunk. Winter crisped the air about her; it even *felt* fresher here, despite Easthill Manor being no more than a twenty-minute carriage ride from Wilmington Bury.

Lady Wilkins appeared in the front doorway, a heavy shawl flung about her shoulders and arms. "Come in, come in, my dear." She waved Belle forward.

Belle did as she was told but didn't relinquish her delight at being once more in her favorite place in all the world. The elegant entryway echoed the rap-rap-rap of servants' feet against the tiled floors. Oh, how she'd dreamed of returning ever since Twelfth Night last year.

She supposed that was rather pathetic of her. But there it was.

"Miss Young." The thick voice of Mrs. Byrd, the housekeeper, broke into her thoughts. "I have ye all set up in your usual bedchamber." She leaned in, her heavyset frame as plump as ever. With a quick glance over at Lady Wilkins, who stood beside the doorway still seeing to the unloading, Mrs. Byrd whispered, "I changed out two of the knickknacks as of late. No one's seemed to be able to figure out just which two. I'm eager to see if ye have any better luck."

"If you truly had wanted to test me," Belle said with an answering smile, "you shouldn't have told me you changed anything out at all."

"Ah, but I didn't tell any o' the maids. Not one of them has said a word. And they're paid to know these sorts of things."

"Then I accept the challenge." Better yet, she would take a couple of things from the room and leave them elsewhere in the house—see if Mrs. Byrd had as sharp an eye as everyone in Easthill Manor believed.

"Don't stand about," Lady Wilkins said, gliding over to where Belle and the housekeeper stood. "I'm sure our sweet Belle wants to rest before dinner." She turned more fully toward Belle, even as Mrs. Byrd curtsied and hurried off. "With the Smith family visiting all the way from America, I must say I'm rather tempted to show off our home in style and keep Town hours."

"I think you could keep any hours you pleased, serve nothing but cold cuts for every meal, skip half the Christmas Eve decorations, and choose a deplorably small yule log and the Smiths would *still* return to America with nothing but awe and adulations for you." How could the Smiths not? Lady Wilkins was a countess and, as such, highly respected by all.

Lady Wilkins shook her head, but her face showed she was clearly pleased. "Nonsense." Looping her arm around Belle's, she tugged her forward, and they began walking up the grand staircase together. "I suppose it is only my pride making me wish to show everything off in the most flattering light." They reached the landing, but Lady Wilkins hesitated instead of continuing down the hallway. "I must confess, country hours are ever so much more comfortable for a woman of my age."

The words made Belle pause. Lady Wilkins did not often speak of her age, yet now she'd done it twice in the past five days. Truth was, Belle half-believed the matron had convinced herself that she was still barely above thirty and had done so with such authority and tenacity that her body had simply complied. Yet, now that Belle took a closer look at her dear friend, she saw wrinkles that had not been there last year and certainly a few dozen more strands of gray hair. It was sobering to see proof that even one so commanding as Lady Wilkins would not be around forever.

Belle hugged the woman's arm closer to her. "You keep whatever hours you want. This is your house and I'm sure the Smiths will accept whatever you decide and be quite pleased all the same."

Lady Wilkins smiled, and a small bit of her regal posture slipped into something more comfortable, if a bit tired-looking. "I had not known we would be having company for the Christmas holidays," she admitted.

Belle secretly tucked away the warmth that came from hearing that Lady Wilkins did not consider *her* as anything nearly so stuffy as "company."

"Did Fezzi not tell you anything?" She could understand him not telling Belle, but to not tell his own mother? Even when she would be expected to plan and prepare for their arrival?

Lady Wilkins shook her head. "He is a dear boy, as we both

know, but not always the most forward-thinking." She gave Belle's hand a quick squeeze. "Now you must excuse me. I have meals to plan and outings to arrange."

"Of course," Belle said, stepping down the hall a bit, intent on removing herself to her bedchamber. "I am sure a houseful is quite a lot of work."

"It is," Lady Wilkins said, hurrying away. "Gracious me, but it is."

Belle, alone in the hallway, let her smile grow to one that was much too big to be considered ladylike, or likely even pretty. But she didn't want to stop smiling. She was at Easthill Manor—the single place on earth that always felt like home. Even Lady Wilkins's mention of the Smith family hadn't dulled her enthusiasm.

Belle ran her hand over the wood paneling along the walls. The trim formed a series of box-shaped inlays—fifteen boxes from floor to ceiling—all down the hallway. The doors were no different and one could only tell where there were doors because *those* boxes were set back a foot and a half, opening up the hallway yet wider at each doorway.

Belle didn't need help finding her room. It was as Mrs. Byrd had said; she stayed in the same room every year, and every year it became hers all over again. The place where she slept, granted. But also, the place where she sipped drinking chocolate in the morning, the place where her abigail fussed over her curls before dinner, the place where she stared through the window and up at the stars on those long nights when she didn't want to sleep.

She pushed the door open. It creaked the exact same cry it had for years. Belle moved into the familiar space. A small fire crackled in the hearth. The curtains were pulled open and the room had clearly been recently dusted. The bedclothes were fresh and felt inviting beneath her fingertips. Her trunks were already in the room and if she had to guess, she would wager that most of her dresses had already been hung in the dressing room off to one side. Her trunk with the puppets rested at the foot of her bed. She would need to pull out the remaining characters and continue her work on them soon if she was to finish in time for the Twelfth Night ball.

Slowly, Belle made her way over to the hearth, hands clasped behind her back. Gracious, but it was good to be back. Even if Miss Smith was in residence—her stomach tightened —Belle was determined not to let the woman dampen her mood. No doubt, now that Belle was at Easthill Manor, she would be able to observe enough to decide on the best course of action.

Her eye caught hold on the strangely empty corner of the mantel. There used to be a little statue of a dog there. She most certainly remembered it.

Mrs. Byrd. Belle smiled and shook her head. She would scour the house and find it—and anything else she'd hidden elsewhere in the manor—and return them to their rightful place. This was Belle's room now, and she would prove herself a very watchful mistress.

Running her fingers over the mantel, she moved closer to the bookcase to the right. Just how well did Mrs. Byrd know the manor? Would she, say, know if a few books had been placed somewhere else?

A loud crash echoed about the hallway, shattering the silence. Belle started, and her heart raced. Whatever could have caused such a sound? She held still and listened, but no cry of pain came next. Neither was there the sound of footsteps hurrying toward the commotion. All was simply still once more. Belle picked her skirt up a bit and stepped out of the room and down the hall. She passed nearly half a dozen other bedchambers; the family wing was quite extensive at Easthill Manor.

At the end of the long hallway, another set of stairs, far

smaller than the grand one she'd come up, extended up to the fourth floor of the house. She wasn't fully sure, but if she had to guess, the crash had come from up there.

Taking hold of the banister, she carefully climbed the steps. The fourth floor was rarely used, she knew. It was more of a place for storing things than it was for living. She moved down another hall, this one unadorned and not nearly so wide. No one seemed to be about at all. None of the bustling of servants or the drifting voices of conversations made it this far. For the first time Belle could remember, she stood inside Easthill Manor in complete silence. Her own soft footfalls padded against the Wilkinson floor; there was no rug here. The ceiling peaked in the center and she was quite certain she was looking up at the very rafters which held the roof of this enormous place.

A single door stood open off to her left. She moved over to it, the narrow hall feeling quite large in its emptiness. Belle ran a hand over her other arm; gooseflesh rose up all down her skin. Whatever had made the noise from before seemed to be keeping entirely still now.

She peered into the room. The peak of the ceiling continued its downward slope making the ceiling near the outer wall far shorter than the wall beside the door and hallway. A few windows lined the far wall, letting in enough daylight that one did not need a candle to see. The room was full of tables and chairs, most of which were stacked neatly atop one another. There were tall chests of drawers and rolled-up rugs. Belle stepped inside, running her fingers atop a well folded and stacked pile of holland clothes.

"Oh good—"

Belle jumped at the voice, a small shriek catching in her throat.

"—it's only you."

She whirled around. James stood halfway behind the door.

"Good heavens," Belle breathed, placing a hand against her collarbone.

James only chuckled in a low, rumbling bass. "Did I scare you?"

How could he not have? "A little," she confessed. Truly, he'd scared her far more than "a little," but she didn't care to admit just how close to jumping out of her own skin she'd come.

He laughed again; the sound was far more captivating than it should have been. Belle very nearly forgot her fright and smiled in spite of herself.

"Then I am sorry." James moved across the room and nearer to her. His jacket was sprinkled with dust, particularly atop his shoulders and near his wrists.

Belle lifted a hand and brushed over his jacket. "What have you been up to?" Specks of dirt flipped into the air at her touch, billowing about and somehow managing to settle on James just as they had been before.

James shrugged. "Just making sure I see all of Easthill Manor before I'm forced to leave after Twelfth Night."

Oh, that couldn't be the whole story at all. With that much dust on him? And what of the crash a few minutes ago? She tipped her head up, eying him with her mouth pulled to one side and a single brow lifted.

He must have seen her unhidden disbelief, for he smiled even wider and shook his head. "Well, perhaps I was doing more than just walking about."

"Clearly." Belle glanced about the room. Now that she looked closer, she could see a couple of cabinet doors had been pulled open, and two different secretaries had drawers hanging out. "What are you looking for?"

In the corner behind James lay a mound of old, rolled-up rugs lying on their side. That, then, had been the crash which had brought her up here. Everything spoke of a man on the hunt: the many footsteps across the dusty floorboards, the doors and drawers hanging open. She returned her gaze to James.

He wasn't smiling anymore. Instead, his expression was quite serious, his mouth in a tight line. He ran a hand over his chin. The easy air of moments ago was gone, replaced with something stiff and uncertain.

"It's nothing," he said, not looking at her.

Belle folded her arms, pinning him down with a stare.

James blew out a long slow breath. "I need...something."

"And you expect to find that something here?"

His only response was a noncommittal grunt.

He clearly didn't want to talk about it—was probably hoping she would leave the room without another word or question. If he'd been Harriet or Aunt Agnes, and they'd been in Wilmington Bury instead of Easthill Manor, she most certainly would have done just that. But here she wasn't a nobody. She wasn't the orphaned child of a title-less gentleman. A woman of standing and respectability wasn't dismissed out of hand.

Belle turned casually about a bit, looking over the organized, if dusty, room. "Tell me what it is and maybe I can help you find it?"

James clearly hesitated. Would he demand she leave? He took two steps away and ran a hand over a large armoire.

He rapped his knuckles over it thrice and then turned and faced her once more. "All right, but under one condition. You speak of this to no one. Not Fezzi, not any of the Smiths. *Certainly* not Lady Wilkins." He added the last part under his breath.

"Why not Lady Wilkins?"

He was hiding something, Belle just wasn't sure what manner of a secret it might be.

He tried to brush off her comment, returning to the far side of the room and stacking the rugs once more.

James was an upstanding gentleman to say the least, so Belle wasn't concerned he was doing anything untoward. But what might he want to keep hidden from—

Then it hit her. "It's a present for her, isn't it?"

James didn't turn around. "Possibly," he said over his shoulder.

It made sense. This was the Christmas season; though gift-giving was not all that common, it wasn't farfetched that a gentleman like James would want a meaningful gift for his aunt and hostess. If any gifts were exchanged, it usually happened on Nicolas Day. However, James had only just returned from America. He most likely hadn't had a chance to purchase his aunt something so soon after his arrival. Moreover, it seemed purchasing her some impersonal trinket was not what he had in mind.

"Tell me then," she said, excitement building inside her once more. "What are we hunting for?"

James placed the last fallen rug in its place and clapped his hands to remove the dust. It was rather pointless, truly, for he was covered already.

Belle stood, ready to help, but waiting for James to respond. Finally, as his silence dragged out, she let out a small, nervous laugh. "I cannot help if you don't tell me what we're looking for. Or would you rather I just walk around and verbalize an inventory of the entire room?"

James still didn't smile, but moved on to a small circular side table, pulling open the little drawer just below the tabletop.

Was he *this* nervous about his Christmas gift? Lady Wilkins could be intimidating at times, especially to those who didn't know her. But underneath her imposing nature, she was just as considerate and kind as anyone Belle knew.

Belle walked over to James, stopping his agitated searching

with a hand on his arm. "I know you care deeply for Lady Wilkins, and for Fezzi."

He stilled and slowly his head swung her way.

"Do you truly believe they will appreciate this gift?" she asked.

"Yes," was his firm answer.

She gave him an encouraging smile. "Then don't fret so. Just tell me how I can help."

"All right." He stood up straight once more. "I'm looking for an old letter. One that was kept by my aunt's previous lady's maid."

"An old letter?" Belle pressed her lips together, her gaze shifting over the room once more. Where might an old letter be kept? Or accidentally placed? "It is a rather odd treasure you are after, sir." Nonetheless, she moved toward one of the secretaries and began looking in each of the small drawers beneath the roll top.

"I understand that," James said, searching yet another side table. "And if you don't care to assist me, I won't be put out."

Did he think she would shirk just because the task was unusual? "After a full Christmas in the same house, one would have thought you knew me better than that."

James paused in his searching for a moment, just long enough to bow most elegantly. "I beg your pardon, my lady," he said in an overly refined tone.

Belle laughed lightly again. On a day like today, even after being scared most thoroughly moments ago, it was hard not to laugh. Moreover, now she was engaged in as diverting a scheme as she'd ever been made a part of. This was promising to be a most wondrous Christmas.

CHAPTER SEVEN

James sat near Lady Wilkins at the long end of the table, but his gaze rarely left Belle, seated near Fezzi at the head. Had he been right in telling her of his quest to find the condemning letter? She'd come to the conclusion herself that it was in an effort to make Lady Wilkins a special, personal Christmas gift. He'd agreed with her assumption though, so he wasn't exactly innocent of lying.

But to protect Fezzi? He didn't feel the least bit of guilt over it. James let his mind wander back to their years at Eton—particularly the first year they'd attended. One of the older boys had decided James was an easy target. Fezzi had stood up to him one afternoon, taking the punches meant for James.

Had he ever told Fezzi how much that had meant to him? It wasn't just that he'd avoided the pummeling, it was knowing he wasn't alone. James had never been alone, not after his mother had passed when he was a boy, nor after his father had done the same some years later.

James would lie to Fezzi himself if it kept him in Easthill Manor—and it looked like he was going to have to. James dropped his gaze to the potato soup in front of him. He placed his spoon inside the bowl, but instead of scooping some to his mouth, he simply swirled the quickly cooling liquid about. This whole ordeal had him fit to be tied. He shifted about in his chair, wishing the tension in his shoulders would abate. It didn't, and it probably wouldn't, not until he found Mr. Thrup and the blasted letter.

Belle laughed at something Fezzi said, pulling his gaze to her once more. Miss Smith laughed, too. It was interesting to hear both women at once. Miss Smith's laugh was boisterous, far more so than most women of the *ton*. It wasn't unpleasant or harsh. Simply robust.

Belle's laughter, though, caught him and held him. It was light—again, not at all like other women James knew—but it wasn't simpering or practiced. It was just...well, melodic. It was sincere, and it suited her. Belle wasn't showy, nor did she demand the attention of the whole room. But when one took the time to notice her, it was hard to miss the fact that she shone brighter than any candle or golden ornament.

He wished he knew what Fezzi was thinking regarding both women. James was under the impression Fezzi had made Belle a promise; but then, why bring Miss Smith to England? A small voice, buried deep inside him, whispered that if Fezzi had no promise with Belle then *James* could possibly—

He stopped the thought before it could finish. He would not pursue Belle, no matter how much her smile lifted him, or how much her laughter called to him. She and Fezzi had far too much history between them for him to step in the middle and expect anything other than ostracism.

Moreover, he had far too much to worry about just now.

"Do you not like potato soup?" Miss Nancy Smith asked, pulling James's attention away from the other end of the table. Dressed in soft purple, and with her hair in two braids running down her back, the young girl looked barely old enough to be out of the nursery.

He glanced at his bowl. The servants had already removed half the bowls along the table, while his own still sat nearly full. It was most certainly cold now, too.

James pushed it away a bit. "I find myself not in the mood for it this evening, that is all," he said.

Miss Nancy nodded as though his answer was as logical as any she'd ever heard. "George gets that way sometimes, too."

The servants cleared both his own bowl and Miss Nancy's. It was replaced with a plate of roast beef and cooked carrots. It smelled heavenly; it was rather a shame he probably wouldn't be able to eat this any more than he'd eaten the soup.

Though Miss Nancy was quite young to be dining with the adults, she held herself upright and spoke clearly while still coming across as demure; she presented herself quite as though she were the diamond of the Season. "George says potatoes don't always agree with her digestion."

"Nancy!" Mrs. Smith hushed her daughter from across the table.

Miss Nancy, however, showed no signs of remorse and instead picked up her fork and knife and cut a small bit of meat off, most daintily.

"Are you pleased with England so far?" James asked, amused that mere seconds after he'd noted the girl's impressive comportment, she'd mentioned her sister's digestion. Still, with his mind elsewhere, he didn't feel like trying to join in the conversation being bantered about nearer the head of the table. Miss Nancy suited him just fine for the time being.

"Quite," came the overly polite reply.

James's mouth pulled to the side. This girl had all the makings of a deuced social splash in a few years.

She continued between graceful bites. "I have found it all quite to my liking."

Why, she hardly sounded American at all. "And what, pray tell, have you found to be the most diverting?" The simple conversation was proving exactly what he needed. A little distraction, but nothing taxing. His eyes jumped to Belle who was eagerly listening to Fezzi telling of some such adventure or another. James most certainly *had* enjoyed her company that afternoon. Having her about had made the search of something no man ever wanted to find far less overwhelming.

"...but, perhaps even more than that," Miss Nancy was saying. James pushed thoughts of his afternoon with Belle aside and returned his mind to the conversation at hand. "I must admit to being relieved at not having George forever speaking about Lord Wilkins."

An uneasiness slipped into the conversation, though James felt certain he was the only one who felt it. "She spoke of Fezzi often on your journey over?"

"Oh, yes." The dear, young girl was already learning how to feign complete boredom and disinterest. Her poor parents. "Every day it was 'Lord Wilkins this' and 'Lord Wilkins that.' I grew quite exhausted at the very sound of his name."

James tried to laugh softly—he felt certain it was the reaction she was hoping for. Yet, he couldn't get it to sound fully natural. Belle had waited far longer than Miss Smith to see Fezzi again. Though Belle didn't have a younger sister to voice her longing to, he had no doubt that she'd felt that same anxious anticipation for the entire three years Fezzi had been away.

Perhaps James should speak to Fezzi on this issue after all. Again, fear that doing so would only inadvertently push Fezzi toward a union surfaced. James had not yet found Mr. Thrup. Thinking the man would suddenly show himself if Fezzi did wed was possibly farfetched. But James was desperate to keep Fezzi safe. He couldn't risk even farfetched uncertainties—not until he learned more.

Miss Nancy had grown silent, her attention taken up in

figuring out how to elegantly cut up the last bit of her meat without appearing like she was sawing the thing in two.

Without conversation to divert him, James couldn't help but let his attention move once more to Belle. She'd made a point of staying near Fezzi all night. She'd even somehow managed to get him to take her into dinner.

There she was, just waiting for Fezzi to wake up and realize what a beauty he already had in her, all the while hoping for their future, wanting him in her life. And what was Fezzi about? Being a bacon-brained twit, that's what.

Fezzi was James's best friend and cousin, besides. But even James had to admit that, when it came to Belle, Fezzi was as blind as an old man in a dark alley. He slowly shook his head. If *he* had someone like Belle looking at him like she was looking at Fezzi right now, he certainly wouldn't be wasting any time. He'd be down on one knee and posting the banns.

A vibrant image of Belle on his arm as they stood in a church before a pastor flashed across his eyes. It was so clear it nearly felt tangible. She was in white, her hand pressed against his arm. She smiled at him, and her whole face shone. Then, equally as fast, it slipped away, and James was only looking at her from down the table once more.

The *feeling* though—that lingered. The bit of heat and passion, the yearning and delight. Gads, a man should *not* be thinking or feeling anything like that in regard to the woman who'd set her cap at his cousin and best friend. James shook himself and sat up straighter.

"Not much in a mind for roast or carrots either?" Miss Nancy asked.

James couldn't help himself—he glanced at the head of the table yet again. Still, Fezzi spoke on; still, Belle watched him as though her very happiness depended on him. In a lot of ways, James knew it did.

And Fezzi was still being a blind idiot.

A fool and a nincompoop.

Fezzi's livelihood—his very way of life—was on the line and he was blissfully unaware. The woman of any man's dreams was sitting beside him, smiling, and he seemed equally unaware of that. Just how much of Fezzi's perfect life would James be forced to hold together for him?

With all that mucking about in a man's brain, who could possibly be in the mood for roast and carrots?

"No," he said at length, finally answering Miss Nancy's question. "I don't suppose I am."

CHAPTER EIGHT

Belle moved away from a large, darkly stained secretary and on to a chest of drawers. No letters. No parchment of any kind. The clanks and bangs of James's equally unfruitful search came from across the room.

"Are you sure there's even something to be found?" she asked. It had been a few days since he'd agreed to let her help, but with Lady Wilkins as their host, they hadn't been granted much free time. Lady Wilkins prided herself on being an excellent host and had, therefore, packed their days rather full.

"I am not," James said, his tone flat as he searched on.

Belle looked about her. There weren't many hiding places left. Her gaze landed on a large oak trunk in the far corner. She had to push a few chairs and a pile of holland clothes out of the way to get to it, but get to it she did. Once the space about it was cleared away, she knelt down and unlatched the large trunk. The lid was heavy, and the metal clasps were cold where they pressed into her palms.

Inside were several baby dresses, still soft and white. Belle aahed as she gently moved one aside and then another. Baby clothes were always so sweet.

James's footsteps echoed about the room as he moved to stand directly behind her. "What's got you all excited suddenly?"

Belle held up one of the littlest dresses, twisting about as she did so to see his reaction.

James only smirked.

Belle pursed her lips and blew out a frustrated breath. "Don't mock me. I think baby things are adorable."

He crouched down, his knees extending out in front of him as he rocked onto the balls of his feet to keep his balance. "I'm not mocking you," he said in a most sincere tone. The sound brought back a rush of half-formed memories. She'd forgotten how much she liked the sound of James's serious-yet-compassionate voice.

"Well," she placed the dress atop another one in the trunk and picked up what had been beneath it, "you *sounded* rather like you were mocking me."

"Never," James said, but then the levity of before resurfaced. "However, I couldn't help but imagine Fezzi, as he is now, dressed in something so frilly as that." He laughed again. The sound came from deep in his chest and the way it rumbled sent new gooseflesh crawling up her arms; it was an alluring delight.

Oh gracious, she was staring at him. Belle forced her gaze away and back to the little dress in her hands. He hadn't noticed, had he? Heat spread over her cheeks. Perhaps if she laughed easily with him—as she had dozens of times in the past—he wouldn't notice. And he was right; Fezzi would look hilarious.

Belle put the dress up against herself. "I think it would make a very handsome cravat, don't you?"

James laughed harder. "What a splash he'd make next season. You should bring the whole trunk down at dinner tonight."

"We'll convince him together." She placed the dress back and pulled out a lacy blanket. "What about this?"

"A sash for across his waistcoat," James supplied.

"Like this?" Belle held one corner atop her left shoulder and the other at her waist. With a flip of her hair, she assumed a most pompous and regal demeanor.

"Not quite." James reached for the corner at her shoulder, his hand still speckled heavily with dust.

Belle pulled back quickly. "Don't touch the blanket."

He rocked back, clearly surprised. "You're touching it."

She tilted her head, blinking innocently. "True. But you see, I'm not the one covered in filth."

"Nonsense." He lunged forward again.

Belle rocked back, holding the small blanket far above her head and away from James. Struggling to keep the perfectly clean cloth away from him, Belle tipped slightly to the side and landed hard on her seat. Still, she didn't lower the blanket.

James crawled forward, reaching over her for it. The deep roll of his laugh mingled with the far lighter sound of hers.

"No." She giggled. "No. You'll get it all dirty."

He leaned forward, his chest hovering over her own. She was out of space. With her dress impeding her retreat and her arms certainly shorter than his, even holding the blanket as far back as she could, his hand was going to snatch it from her. There was no avoiding it. The poor, dear baby blanket would be ruined.

Then suddenly, he paused.

His eyes met hers, and they both grew still.

He was so close, yet she didn't know a want for space. His eyes were a deep, inviting shade of blue. She could see his kindness, but also his merriment for life.

What did he see in her eyes?

Then his head twisted, and he looked over his shoulder; best she could tell, he was looking toward the door. Belle held her breath for a moment, shaking off the strange and unexpected pull.

A noise sounded from outside; no doubt it was the very thing that had drawn James's attention.

Steps on the stairs. "A maid?" Belle whispered.

Jumping back, James took hold of both her arms and all but tossed her up into the air as he helped her stand.

"Hide," he whisper-yelled.

They dashed back behind the door. James pulled her down behind a large stack of chairs. Belle bent down, trying to fold herself into as small a ball as possible. James's arm was across her shoulders, and he was pressed up against her side. His chest still heaved heavily from their laughter and game of moments ago.

Never had she been so close to a man. Granted, they were both trying to hide behind a stack of chairs which would normally be considered only big enough for one of them. Still, Belle was quite aware of the comfortable way his arm rested across her back, of his hand on the ground near hers, and of his lips close to her ear. The same pull from before tingled across her skin once more. Which was silly. James was Fezzi's cousin.

Neither of them said a thing, but both silently watched the back side of the door.

The footfalls grew louder, and a soft humming accompanied it. A young maid moved into the room and her soft song grew louder. It wasn't one Belle recognized, but it was melodious and pleasing to hear all the same. The maid turned her back toward Belle and James, picked up a small, framed picture, and then moved back out again without so much as glancing their way.

Belle breathed out a sigh of relief.

James must have felt the same for he leaned back against the wall and seemed to relax, his eyes closing.

Come to think of it... "James," she asked, with a soft chuckle, "why were we hiding?" She'd gone along with him in the moment, but now, looking back, it seemed rather unnecessary. Yes, they were alone in the room, but the door was open. Moreover, here at Easthill Manor, Belle was family. So was James. Nothing untoward would happen and everyone knew it. They'd most certainly been as alone as this more than once three years ago.

James still didn't open his eyes, but silently shook his head. The joy was gone from his expression; she didn't need to see his eyes to know that. The seriousness she'd seen in him a few times these past days had returned. She didn't know what was causing it, but it was evident all the same.

"You must truly want this to be a surprise," Belle said, "if you're even going so far as to keep it from the servants."

His eyes opened and she saw exactly what she expected. A dark, weighty concern tossed and turned in his blue eyes. "Secrecy is imperative."

Where was the laughing, lighthearted James? She always seemed to miss him whenever this troubled, uncertain James showed up.

"I suppose," she said but he truly needn't be so concerned over a Christmas gift.

"Belle." He reached for her. "I'm seri—"

Belle tugged her hand away, smiling. "Don't touch me, you dirty hog."

It did the trick. The seriousness in his eyes gave way to humor. "Dirty hog? Have you looked over yourself?"

Belle glanced down, then twisted about trying to better see herself. She was nearly as dust-covered as he was. "My abigail will have words for you, most certainly."

"So will the scullery maid when she goes to wash our clothes." He stood and offered her a hand.

Belle placed hers inside his. "They may call you out for such debauchery."

His brows dropped, all mock solemnity. "Do I have any chance at survival?"

"None, whatsoever," she declared. "Best set your estate in order and notify your next of kin."

He nodded. "You can hold the funeral on Christmas Day."

"Why then?"

"That would save cook from needing to organize and prepare yet another large feast."

"You expect your funeral to be well attended, do you?"

"Of course. Any man who is willing to die at such a time as to make it easier on the household by corresponding such an event with another large, pre-planned gathering should understandably be well-mourned."

Belle patted him in the chest with both hands. "Magnanimous, thy name is James Radcliff." She felt his laughter beneath her palms.

James wrapped a hand around both of hers, keeping them in place. "There is one thing we've forgotten, however."

"Oh?" something about his hand holding hers against his chest changed the way the air around her felt. It hummed, filling with heated awareness.

"I believe you owe it to me to stand in as my second."

"Who, me?"

"You did appoint yourself my companion in all this." He spread his other arm out, indicating the room and all they'd searched through.

"True."

"I think it only fair you stand in."

"Against my abigail and the scullery maid? I wouldn't dare." The pull between them was proving too much and she couldn't stop herself from leaning in ever so much closer.

The light in his eyes shifted, moving from lighthearted and

teasing, to serious. But not heavy; not as it had been. "I really am glad you're helping me with this, Belle."

The hand holding hers dropped down, though James didn't let go. He turned and stepped forward. They moved across the room, her hand still inside his.

"You've made this whole ordeal far easier," James said.

"You consider searching out a late Christmas present an ordeal?"

He gave her hand a quick squeeze then let go. "Just know I'm glad you're here."

CHAPTER NINE

*I*t was St. Nicolas Day—one of the days Belle most looked forward to every year. Traditionally, they spent the day sledding. Then there would be a warm fire and an excellent dinner. The evening would conclude with snapdragon and they'd all finally head off to bed far later than usual.

But this year, though she was most excited at the prospects the day held, Belle's thoughts repeatedly drifted away from the season and toward James instead. She hadn't fully shaken the feel of her hand inside his. Even more so, she couldn't seem to stop thinking back to when he'd knelt above her, reaching for the blanket. Or that moment when they'd had to hide, and he'd pulled her in close to him. The incident had taken place the day before last, yet the rush of his touch still echoed about inside of her as though it had only just happened. Belle pushed her arm into the sleeve of her spencer. Thinking back on that moment was naught but childish—a silly giddiness which only illuminated her own naivety. James was a friend, but he wasn't Fezzi. Moreover, James had only held her close because they were hiding—right?

The jacket pulled strangely across the back and Belle refocused her mind on the present. She'd pulled the spencer on upside down. She shook her head; what a nodcock thing to do. At least she was alone in her bedchamber and not where Fezzi could see her. Or Miss Smith. The last thing Belle needed right now was that woman laughing at her.

As Belle twisted about, trying to disentangle herself from the spencer, her gaze traveled over the trunk that held her puppets. For a moment, she stilled. She was inexcusably behind on her various creations. Truly, she was quite vexed with herself. She supposed she could cry off sledding, stay home for the day, and work hard on getting everything ready for her Twelfth Night performance.

However, Belle had been trying for days to garner more attention from Fezzi. He didn't seem to be annoyed or in any way avoiding her, but he didn't seem very keen on her either. Finally working the spencer off, she righted it and once more pulled her arms through the sleeves. Well, today provided her with the perfect opportunity; she would just have to find a way to speak to Fezzi alone. The puppets could wait.

She *did* pick up a small knickknack from the bedside table. She would place it in the foyer and see if Mrs. Byrd noticed. At least she still had time for that.

Sledding on St. Nicolas Day had always been something she and Fezzi had done together. Surely he wouldn't let Miss Smith ruin their tradition. Perhaps if they had a few minutes just to themselves she could remind him how well they'd always gotten along. Remind him that they *would* be happy together.

A sure thing such as their camaraderie and friendship was not to be taken lightly. He surely knew that, surely remembered what he'd promised.

Belle closed her eyes just briefly. She'd never again have to be told by Harriet that she was a nobody, a forgotten castaside.

Belle moved over to the mirror and checked that all was in place. She was already growing warm in the long-sleeved dress, quilted spencer jacket, extra thick gloves, and fur-lined bonnet —a gift from Lady Wilkins for today's outing. Once she added her pelisse on top of it all she was surely going to roast if they didn't step outside soon.

Her cheeks looked a bit flushed—proof she was overheating. Either that, or proof that she was growing increasingly frustrated, and alarmed, at Fezzi's clear lack of interest in her.

Even more complicated, perhaps it was just proof that she hadn't fully forgotten her moments alone with James on the fourth floor.

Turning, she rested her back against the wall beside the mirror. His moods had been a bit off as of late. Most of the time, he was his expected, happy, considerate self. Yet there were moments, such as when they'd nearly been caught looking for old letters, when his eyes belied his happiness. Instead, she'd seen unmistakable concern and worry. What was putting it there?

At first, she had assumed it had something to do with his estate; that was why he had returned to England ahead of Fezzi, after all. But then, why be so afraid of being caught on the fourth floor by a young maid? And he *had* been far too hesitant to accept her help if he truly was only searching out a present for Lady Wilkins.

No, he had to be hiding something from her.

Belle stood straight and looked herself over in the mirror. All seemed put to rights, so she left and crossed quickly down the hall and stairs toward the front door. Today, she would try to tackle *two* obstacles: garner a bit more of Fezzi's attention, and see if she couldn't begin to piece together what was troubling James.

If they all had an enjoyable day sliding down snowy hills while she was at it, so much the better.

James pulled his greatcoat tighter around his shoulders and stepped outside. Fezzi and Belle were already there, speaking in low tones. He was happy to admit, though he knew full well that Belle wanted Fezzi's attention and even an offer from him, she'd never once become clingy, needy, or any of the other things women of the *ton* so often did when vying for a man.

James took the steps slowly, one at a time. Between Miss Smith dominating every conversation she entered, and Belle's insistence that she help him with Lady Wilkins's "Christmas gift," James figured Fezzi and Belle hadn't had nearly enough time together. He wasn't going to intrude now.

As he stepped onto the snow-covered ground, Belle glanced his way. The moment his gaze caught hers, he felt an ever-more-familiar heat rush over him. She smiled, and he couldn't help but smile in return.

Her gaze returned to Fezzi, and James felt the cold of the morning once more.

"Come now, Mother," cried out a girlish voice—one very nearly British but still clearly not. "I've never gone sledding *in England*; suppose it's not at all like sledding at home?"

James turned back toward Easthill Manor's grand door. It was open, and none other than Miss Nancy stood in it, draped in a large coat which was clearly two sizes too big, flatly refusing to heed her mother, who stood beside her with only a shawl around her shoulders; the woman already shivered against the cold.

"It's too cold, Nancy," Mrs. Smith said, waving her daughter back inside.

"I have a warm coat."

A maid appeared in the doorway behind Mrs. Smith, a large thick blanket hanging between her hands. She offered it to Mrs. Smith, but the older woman only shooed the maid away. "Nancy, I insist you come back inside this minute before we both catch our death of cold."

"Please, Mama." Nancy's voice dropped the bit of British it had acquired as of late and turned decidedly American.

"Inside. Now."

Poor Miss Nancy. She looked close to tears. James hated to see the young girl so upset. It was Christmas, after all. What was that if not a time for trips through a snow-graced forest? He hurried up the steps, taking them two at a time. Miss Nancy looked ready to head in, but then caught sight of James. Her eyes were full of such hope, he hated to disappoint her.

He took the blanket from the maid who still hovered in the doorway, clearly unsure what to do. Shaking it out, he draped it over Mrs. Smith's shoulders.

"If you are worried for her safety," he said, "I can keep an eye on her."

Mrs. Smith pursed her lips then turned toward James. "I'd hate for her to be a bother."

"She would be no bother at all, I assure you."

Miss Nancy was dutifully silent, but her eyes sparkled as her gaze jumped from him to her mother and back again.

With a loud sigh, Mrs. Smith closed her eyes. "All right, then. You may go, Nancy."

Miss Nancy let out a short squeal.

"Be sure you stay close to Mr. Radcliff," her mother instructed.

Miss Nancy nodded furiously.

James had no sisters, no brothers either, but he'd often wondered what it would have been like to have a sibling. Fezzi complained often enough about his sister, Eliza. But perhaps having a sister wouldn't have been nearly as bad as his cousin made it out to be. Particularly, if, unlike Eliza, the sister had been younger than he and as sweet at Nancy. Stepping forward, James extended his arm to Miss Nancy.

With a prim smile any matron would have complimented, she slipped her arm through his.

"Thank you," Mrs. Smith said softly.

James tipped his hat and she stepped back inside.

"Now," James said to the young girl, "you stick with me and I'll show you all the best hills for a sled."

"You?" Belle called out.

She and Fezzi were no longer talking, but instead watching him and Miss Nancy. Fezzi seemed only mildly interested, but Belle watched him with an ardor that made his heart skip a beat.

"Of course." He tried to ignore the heat that rushed over him once more. "I am quite adept at finding the perfect hill." He turned back toward the girl on his arm; perhaps if he didn't look directly at Belle, his equilibrium would settle. "Such a hill requires not only a steep side, but also a less steep side for climbing back up."

"Smooth snow is, certainly, a very important aspect as well," Belle added.

How well he remembered her professing just such a thing three years ago. "Are you bamming me? I thought the hill I picked out last time was superb."

Belle tilted her head, trying to appear innocent. "Oh, is that why we rode down it *once* and all quickly agreed *my* hill was the superior choice?"

"It wasn't *your* hill. If anything, these hills belong to Fezzi. He's the master of the land."

Belle dropped the fake-innocence. "We all almost died on the hill you suggested."

He remembered that day so clearly. Belle was not nearly so outspoken as many women—Miss Smith came to mind—but when she put her mind to something, she was not easily persuaded otherwise.

"If I remember correctly," James said, taking a step closer to her, "you claimed not to mind being covered in snow." She'd been breath-taking, speckled in white. At least James had enough wits about him to keep *that* part of the memory to himself.

Belle's eyes glinted with hidden mirth. "I *do* enjoy the snow."

Fezzi broke in for the first time. "What makes you say it like that? What happened?"

Belle's brow creased; she was most becoming when confused. "Don't you remember?"

"How could I?" Fezzi countered, sounding a might put out. "I wasn't there. I had to stay home and see to some tenant business."

"Oh," Belle said slowly. "That's right."

Miss Nancy tugged on James's arm. He leaned in toward her a bit and she whispered, "What *did* happen?"

He gave her a wide smile. "This." In one fluid motion, he scooped up a handful of snow, packed it into a ball as he stood, and then lobbed it Belle's direction.

But Belle was too fast. She ducked behind Fezzi, holding him in front of her like a shield. The ball of snow struck Fezzi across the arm.

"Come now," Fezzi said, brushing the snow off and not losing an ounce of dignity in the process. "We are rather grown for such things, are we not?"

Just then, a snowball sailed out of Belle's hand, over Fezzi's shoulder and hit James squarely in the chest. Thanks to his greatcoat, James felt the impact but none of the cold.

"Now who's covered in snow?" she said, her words mixed with laughter.

"Still a dab hand, I see." He ducked down, reaching for more snow.

Miss Nancy had let go of his arm and now dragged her own two hands through the snow, picking up the largest ball of it he'd ever seen.

"That's the spirit," he said, cheering her on.

Fezzi, still standing ramrod straight, looked around at them all. "What's gotten into you—"

"Best move," James called, waiting for the right moment to strike against Belle. "Or else I guarantee you'll be covered before you can say 'Humbug.'"

Fezzi shook his head and started moving off toward the front steps.

"*Humbug?*" Belle asked, staying rooted to the spot. "Where did you hear a strange term like that?"

James threw the snowball in his hands instead of answering. Belle skipped to the left and the ball only caught the back of her pelisse. Without another word, she dashed for cover behind the side of the manor. Miss Nancy's large snowball trailed after her, but never hit. Instead, it landed atop Belle's footprints with a *plop*.

James scooped up more snow and leaned back, ready to throw.

"We're ready to go now," a voice called from the doorway.

James paused, arm still in the air, and glanced back. Miss Smith stood beside Fezzi.

"You look lovely," Fezzi said, extending his arm toward her.

Miss Smith rested one hand against his arm, and then her other hand as well. Though she wasn't exactly clutching him in talons, the way Miss Smith held onto Fezzi did rather put James in mind of a bird-of-prey.

"Nancy," Miss Smith said, her tone far more clipped than before. "If you're going to join us, I expect you to act like a refined young lady."

Miss Nancy dropped the packed snow in her hands. "He started it," she said, pointing at James.

Traitor.

"Don't point." Miss Smith pushed Miss Nancy's hand back down. "Now, no more childish distractions. I'm ready, and we should be on our way before the day grows any later."

Together, Miss Smith and Fezzi moved stately toward the waiting carriage, equipped with runners instead of wheels, made especially for traveling over winter snow.

The air, which had been full of laughter moments ago, was now sadly still. James turned toward Belle. He half-expected her to be stalking up on him, snowball in hand, ready to deal him a last, fatal blow. But instead, she stood, wordless, looking down at the snow in her hands. Peeling her fingers back one by one, she let the snow fall from her palm. She wasn't smiling. Something shifted behind her eyes, but what, exactly, James couldn't say.

Had Miss Smith's words offended her? She didn't appear angry, not even put out, really. Just sad.

James held his arm out to Miss Nancy, who took it, allowing him to lead her to the carriage. He didn't hurry. Miss Smith's voice floated to him; she was already claiming dominance over the conversation before half the occupants were even seated.

He and Miss Nancy were between Belle and the carriage, and he kept his pace slow so that she'd catch up. As Belle moved closer to him, he extended his free arm to her. She took it but didn't say anything.

He tucked the arm she held closer to himself, drawing her nearer, even as he leaned her way. "You *are* a dab hand at snowball fights."

Belle didn't smile as he'd hoped. Instead, she only shook her head. "I shouldn't be so childish."

Is that what she thought? His gaze jumped to Miss Smith, sitting in the open carriage, her voice carrying to them easily.

"I'm as giddy as a kitten tipping over a milk pail," she said with a broad smile. "It's been *ages* since I've gone sledding and never in England." Her eyes rolled upward. "Obviously." She giggled at her own joke.

"Your sister mentioned as much," Fezzi replied.

Is that what Belle understood Miss Smith to have meant? That anyone who partook of a snowball fight was childish? James handed Miss Nancy up into the carriage, then turned to face Belle fully.

She wasn't frowning, per se, but neither was she smiling. Her eyes looked frightfully dull, too. None of the spark he'd enjoyed moments ago remained. He wished he could tell her that she *wasn't* childish. That Miss Smith was only self-conscious of a little sister joining them. That even if Miss Smith *did* consider snowball fighting beneath her, it was her own loss and not something Belle should heed at all.

But they were standing directly beside the others now. And though Miss Smith's constant chatter would most likely cover any whispered conversation, James didn't want to risk embarrassing Belle further.

Instead, he simply handed her up into the carriage then silently made his own way in.

Only one person inside the open carriage talked the entire duration, and James couldn't help but be struck by the stark differences between Christmases past and the one he was living now.

CHAPTER TEN

Well, she'd most certainly failed at her first objective: to garner more of Fezzi's attention. Belle trudged up the stairs. Heavenly wafts of roasting ham and cooked pecans filled the house, beseeching her to enjoy the festive smell. But Belle couldn't find it in herself to be pleased by the merriment. Miss Smith and Miss Nancy had already scaled the many steps, having rushed past her at the bottom. Belle was relieved to finally have a moment of silence.

Two vexing realizations had come from the day's sledding. The first was that Fezzi seemed to enjoy women who talk incessantly—one thing Belle never saw herself becoming—and two, she could find no worse fault than that to lay against Miss Smith. Yes, she was chatty and left no one guessing her opinions. But she was in no way petty or prone to gossip. She was polite to the manservants who helped them with the sleds and was nothing but amiable to Belle.

If she was painfully honest with herself, there was a third far more vexing realization. Belle was undeniably jealous of Miss Smith. She knew the sentiment was wicked; Aunt Agnes saw that she attended church weekly, and so Belle was not ignorant to the vices of jealousy and the like. Still, she couldn't force the emotion away.

Belle paused at the landing, anxious to be in her own bedchamber, yet struggling to find the strength to climb another set of stairs. She had not missed the way Fezzi had attended to Miss Smith's every need. He'd pulled her sled up the hill for her every time. He'd helped her onto it and then helped her off at the bottom. A dull ache formed in her chest. What she wouldn't give to be the recipient of that kind of attentive kindness.

Suppose she truly was too childish for Fezzi to ever think of her? Suppose he'd forgotten his promise, or worse, remembered and no longer cared?

"That was quite the excursion." James came up and stood beside her.

Belle nodded, taking another step forward, one step closer to her own piece of Easthill Manor—her bedchamber and, unfortunately, one step closer to the next flight of stairs. Why was it that life forever filled one with hope for something grand which *should* come, yet always required one to work so tirelessly for it?

"Are you well?" James asked.

She must not be doing as fine a job hiding her self-doubts as she'd hoped. Belle turned her face toward James; hopefully a small smile and a simple answer would allay his concerns. The moment she saw him—his soft blue eyes and the sincere concern there—all her worry and uncertainty welled up. Dropping her head, she blinked several times.

"Oh, Belle." His arm wrapped around her shoulders, and he pulled her into a sideways hug.

"I promise I'm not a ninny," she said, her words breaking.

"You most certainly are not." They continued forward, taking the next staircase, their footfalls in step.

"It's only, this Christmas has not turned out exactly as I

anticipated." She felt she needed to tell him some excuse or another, and that was as far as she could go without fully humiliating herself.

"I know," he said.

"I'm such a dolt."

"You mustn't say such things." With his arm still wrapped across her shoulders, he began to rub her arm.

"I fear it's true."

"Why is that?"

Because she was vying for the attentions of a man who couldn't seem to remember when she was in the room. Because she was here as an act of charity on Lady Wilkins's part. Because she didn't truly belong to the Wilkins family, or among her own relatives either.

To admit that even those who were honor-bound to care for her did so most begrudgingly, well, it was too demeaning to even speak of.

"Let me ask you this instead," James said at length. They reached the third-floor landing, but still, James's arm didn't fall away from her. "Why are Fezzi's attentions so important?"

An acutely uncomfortable feeling crept over Belle. She couldn't describe it, couldn't name it, but it was like small thorns catching at her skin and pricking her all over.

"A woman must marry," she said, barely louder than a whisper.

"Yes, of course," James capitulated. Blessedly, his tone was neither condemning, nor judgmental. He didn't press her for a more exact answer, but neither did he leave her side. That alone did more to calm her misgivings than anything else he could have done.

"I was hoping," James said, "that you might be of a mind to help me again this evening?"

"Tonight?" Belle dropped her voice low and glanced about, but they were alone in the hallway. "After the evening's festivities, I have no doubt we will all be quite ready to turn in."

"I know, and if you do not feel up to it, then I understand."

Oh, but she hated to abandon him when she might be of some help. It wasn't as though she felt her help amounted to much, but he'd been an ever-dependable friend and telling him no felt cruel.

"In truth, I think a distraction might be exactly what I need," she said. Perhaps, despite failing at her first objective, she could still make some progress toward her second: getting closer to figuring out what James was truly after. "Tell me, had you hoped to give her the gift today?" St. Nicolas Day was a common time for family members to exchange presents.

James didn't answer right away; instead, he rocked his head back and forth before saying, "My task is most urgent."

His "task," was it? How interesting. "Tell me," she said, trying another line of questioning, "why do you not just go into town and purchase a gift from the lovely shops there? You would have plenty of time this afternoon."

"It is like you said before, I find myself in want of something more personal."

"But if we do not find this old letter soon, it will be too late, I fear." If only she understood why he insisted this matter was urgent.

"Yes, but I feel, in this situation, that providing the *right* gift is far better than a *timely* gift."

They reached her door, and both came to a stop in front of it.

"Then why press on tonight," Belle asked, "when we are both sure to be exhausted? Why not wait until after Boxing Day to continue?" They would most certainly be quite busy for the next few days.

"If you want to cry off—"

Belle pulled out of his side hug. "You must not think very much of me if you assume I wish to cry off."

"It's not that—"

Roundabout questions were getting her nowhere. "Are you still going to insist"—she folded her arms as she spoke and sent him her most pressing glare—"that we're looking for an old letter so you can make Lady Wilkins a Christmas gift?"

He rested a hand against the wall to the side of her door. With a sigh, he leaned against it, dropping his head. "No."

"Why did you lie to me?"

"We are dealing with the most delicate of situations. Please believe me."

"You feel I couldn't be trusted to keep a secret? Or that my female sensibilities are too weak for me to know the truth?"

His head came back up. "No. Nothing could be further—"

"Then what?" In her exasperation, she very nearly stomped.

But James's expression truly held regret, as well as uncertainty. Was he uncertain about what he'd done? Or about whether he should have let her help him at all?

"I thought we were friends," she whispered. Finding out that he didn't trust her stung worse than when Miss Smith had insinuated that she was a child for enjoying a snowball fight.

He reached for her, placing his hands against each of her arms. "Never think we aren't friends." His thumbs rubbed circles just below her shoulders. His eyes took in the whole of her face; he seemed eager, nearly starved to know that she understood what he was saying. "Your friendship is most precious to me."

The warmth in his words placed a smile across her face. Never had anyone made her feel so wanted, so important. When she was with James, it was as though it didn't even matter that father had held no title and left her no dowry.

"I need you to believe me," he continued. "I didn't tell you not because I fear you can't keep a secret, or that you are too weak to know the truth. I didn't tell you because it's not my secret to tell."

"Then whose——" Oh. "Lady Wilkins."

James nodded. "This does concern my aunt, and it is out of a deep affection for her that I cannot tell you the whole of it."

They were looking for a letter kept by Lady Wilkins's previous lady's maid. He had to be looking for the information expressed in the letter. "You're looking to learn about something in the past."

"Please, Belle." James's tone turned pleading. "Don't ask more of me. I know you love Lady Wilkins as well, so for her sake, let this rest."

She did love Lady Wilkins. The woman was the closest thing Belle had to a mother—albeit one she rarely saw outside of the winter holidays, for all the matron's frequent trips to London.

Do something for Lady Wilkins? Belle would do anything for her.

"All right, then," she said. "I promise to not ask more questions."

"Thank you." The words rushed out of him with an ardor which immediately hushed all feelings of uncertainty she had been feeling. She trusted James.

"But promise me you'll worry less?" she said.

His lips twisted to the side in an uncertain smile.

When he didn't say anything to the contrary, however, Belle added, "Together, I am certain we will find what you seek. We *will* help Lady Wilkins."

CHAPTER ELEVEN

"I know what we need," Miss Smith decreed from her seat at the long, well-laid dinner table.

Everyone turned her way. All were in attendance at tonight's grand St. Nicolas feast. Mr. Smith and his wife sat on Lady Wilkins's right, at the long end. Their daughters sat across from them on Lady Wilkins's left. Fezzi sat at the head with Miss Smith to one side and James to the other.

Belle was planted most squarely between the two groups, with no one directly across from her. The plates had been spread out along the opposite side of the table, so it wasn't largely apparent. At least Belle hoped she was the only one who had noticed. She couldn't help but feel quite misplaced. Though she could hear both groups conversing, she felt part of neither.

"Well," Mrs. Smith pressed her daughter, "do speak on."

Miss Smith's gaze moved from person to person, clearly wanting to be sure she had the full attention of the room. "We need a *Buche de Noel*."

Every member of the Smith family immediately smiled and quickly turned to their neighbor to delineate the undeniable fact that their old family receipt was, in fact, the best there was to be had. That was to say, the two youngest Smith girls giggled between themselves, Mr. and Mrs. Smith spoke animatedly to Lady Wilkins, and Miss Smith insisted to both Fezzi and James that making their own Buche de Noel would be just the thing.

Belle pushed a bit of ham around her plate. Toward the beginning of dinner, she'd tried to join in the conversation. But Miss Smith's rather elaborate tale of a local butcher's lost cow required little from anyone. After that, Belle had tried to join in the other conversation happening to her left. But the two matrons were discussing what it was like to have adult children. Though Belle tried to appear sympathetic and interested, it wasn't as though she knew anything about the topic herself.

The various voices swirled around her. Still, she did nothing but shift her food around. She was too tired to continue pushing herself on these people. Miss Smith was looking decidedly angelic this evening, dressed as she was in a soft blue and white lace. Belle's own muslin felt quite drab in comparison.

Gracious, if they didn't care one whit if she was present or not, why had they even invited her this year? She would have been just as well off if she'd spent the past few weeks at Wilmington Bury. Her fork's tines clinked against her plate lightly. Good heavens, she was shaking. How humiliating. She must not have fully recovered from her bout of blue-devilment earlier that afternoon. Belle rested her fork ever so carefully down atop the table once more.

Slipping both her hands onto her lap, Belle sat and let the cheerful voices around the table wash over her, but she couldn't find it in herself to care enough to focus on what was being said.

James, sitting directly to her right, reached a hand underneath the table where no one would see and wrapped his fingers around her own. His touch stilled some of the churning emotions inside her.

Leaning closer to her, he whispered low, while maintaining an air of listening to Miss Smith's continued insistence that they make a Buche de Noel that very evening. "Chin up; she can't talk forever."

Belle silenced her most unladylike guffaw only just in time. "So you claim."

The corners of his lips twitched in a ghost of a smile. "So I *hope*, you mean." His fingers gave hers a soft squeeze. "You look lovely tonight."

The kind compliment, spoken so sincerely, undid her. The room around Belle blurred and she quickly blinked away the sudden rush of tears.

James's brow dropped and he turned in his seat, facing her more directly. "Belle?"

She shook her head. "Do not worry. I am only a little tired, is all." Belle glanced around, but no one besides James seemed to be any the wiser to her sudden inability to keep her emotions under control.

"I am sorry," she spoke on. "Perhaps it is best if I retire early." She placed her free hand against the table, meaning to stand.

But James gripped her other hand more fully in his own, and she paused.

"I wouldn't wish you to do anything you don't desire," he said in a rush, "only don't leave just yet."

"James, please," she said. "I feel it is best if I leave before inadvertently making a scene."

His gaze held hers. "I would dearly love it if you stayed."

Perhaps it was the exhaustion, or the ever-growing realization of how little she belonged at Easthill Manor after all, but whatever the cause, Belle looked back at James, and any ladylike revulsions to being straightforward washed away.

"Why?" she said, her tone a bit more demanding than she'd intended.

James's eyes widened slightly. He dropped her hand and rocked back in his chair. "Well..."

Even he couldn't seem to want her. James—whom she considered a good friend, who had laughed with her and told her she wasn't a ninny or childish—couldn't find a reason to wish her around.

Tears pricked against her eyes once more. What rotten timing; if she didn't remove herself from the room immediately, she would be seen crying by all.

Belle made to stand, but the sound of Miss Smith's chair grating loudly against the floor stopped her.

"Come, Fezzi," Miss Smith ordered. "You too, Mr. Radcliff and Miss Young. We are off to make our own Buche de Noel. I have made it so many times, I do believe I could do it with my eyes closed."

Both matrons heartily agreed with Miss Smith's suggestion. Fezzi readily stood. He hadn't glanced at Belle all night. It stung and yet...

And yet it was not so bad as watching James fidget in his chair, unable to tell her why he wished for her to stay.

No, she had no desire to participate tonight. She was probably being petty and silly and overly dramatic, but she couldn't find the strength inside of her to care about the Christmas gaieties.

"You'll have to excuse me," she began. "But I think I will turn in." She needed something to take her mind off the horrid mess this year's winter was turning in to. Mrs. Byrd had found the books Belle had moved from her bedchamber and returned them far sooner than she'd anticipated. She'd also placed a few other books that belonged in the library. Perhaps Belle would return the misplaced books and then search out something else in her bedchamber for Mrs. Byrd to hunt; at the moment, doing so sounded like the perfect distraction.

"Turn in?" Miss Smith asked, aghast. "It's not yet nine o'clock and on St. Nicolas Day, too. No, you shall make a cake with us." She rounded the table and took hold of Belle's arm, pulling her to her feet. "Trust me, a little chocolate will be just the thing. We shall bake it all tonight, and then it'll be ready for tomorrow. There's no better way to celebrate the birth of the Holy Child than with a chocolate cake, you know."

It seemed Belle would not be granted an escape. Instead, Miss Smith pulled her out of the room, down the hall, and toward the back of the manor. Fezzi and James followed behind. Miss Smith spoke on about the details of the task they were about to undertake.

The kitchen was empty and dark when they arrived.

"I nearly forgot," Fezzi said from behind her as they all looked into the open room. "My mother has given nearly all the staff the night off."

"Pish," Miss Smith said. "We won't need them." She stepped into the room a bit, pulling Belle with her. "We will need light though."

"Cook's candles are in that drawer, there." Belle pointed Miss Smith in the right direction.

However, once Miss Smith had pulled a few out, she only wrinkled her nose. "These are rushlights." She turned large doe-eyes on Fezzi. "I'd hate for the smell to ruin our cake."

"Never you fear," Fezzi said, slapping James on the back, "we'll round up enough candles to light the entire space before a man can say Jack Robinson."

James and Fezzi left to find the needed candles, Miss Smith quickly following behind.

Alone in the nearly dark kitchen, Belle felt herself relax for the first time since dinner had begun. What a fool she'd been to think she could turn Fezzi's head. She was plain, simply attired, and not at all engaging as was Miss Smith.

In the very dim light of only two short candles—the ones they'd brought from the dining room—Belle felt her way around the kitchen and found a stool. She pushed it up toward a long table in the center of the room and sat.

Harriet had the right of it, after all. Now that Fezzi had seen more of the world, he clearly realized he could do better than her.

JAMES FOUND HALF A DOZEN OTHER CANDLES IN THE BILLIARD room and hurried back toward the kitchen. He and Fezzi had separated soon after leaving the kitchen, each searching a different part of the house for better light. It was a tad strange to wander through the manor and not see a single footman or maid. He was glad that the servants had been given the evening off—they deserved a nice St. Nicolas Day too—but it still felt strange.

He entered the kitchen to find Belle sitting at the table alone. His step slowed. She didn't look up, didn't appear to have heard his return at all. Her elbow rested atop the table, and she had planted her chin most heavily in her upturned palm. Soft curls fell around her face, having escaped her simple coiffure. The two candles, neither far from her, spilled dancing light across her features. Her eyes looked sad. Despondent.

James fought the urge to go to her and wrap her in his arms as he had so foolishly done that afternoon. The desire to hold her grew markedly stronger by the day. But to act on it would surely spell the end of their friendship.

She was hoping for a connection with Fezzi. He *knew* this. Yet, his heart refused to accept that as adequate reasoning for keeping his distance. When he'd seen her so distraught on the stairs that afternoon, he hadn't stopped himself in time. He'd responded out of a sincere desire to help, it was true, but also because of an equally strong desire to just be near her. The truth was, Belle was the only bright spot in his life right now. Between the weight of Lady Wilkins's secret and his responsibility to his family, he felt quite like he was drowning at times. He needed Belle's constant hope.

She still had not noticed him. He shouldn't be staring at her. It was not at all what a true gentleman would do. But she seemed to need some time to compose herself, and he feared if he made his presence known, he wouldn't be able to stop himself from holding her hand or putting an arm around her.

His gaze dropped to her lips. Or worse.

Closing his eyes, James silently took two long steps backward. Turning, he pressed his back against the wall, making sure he was completely out of view of the kitchen.

Devil take him—what was he doing? Falling for the one woman he knew had no interest in him whatsoever. And falling, he most certainly was. Slowly, he let himself slide down the wall until he was sitting on the floor, his knees propped up.

Then she'd gone and asked him most pointedly why he'd wished her to stay a bit longer tonight. James leaned his head back until it rested against the wall behind him.

Why did he want her around?

Because she was clever and engaging. Because she was witty and easy to talk to. James cared greatly for Fezzi, but that didn't mean he found much enjoyment spending an evening watching his cousin agree to everything a talkative female said.

No—even more than that—he'd simply grown inarguably partial to having Belle around.

Of course, he couldn't have said any of that to her, not with a room full of people far too close to guarantee he wouldn't have been overheard. James set the candles down beside him and ran a hand through his hair.

He would have to stand and walk into the kitchen soon; he couldn't sit out in the hallway all night. It would probably be better if he attempted it before either Fezzi or Miss Smith returned. He'd hate to have to explain to them why he was sitting on the floor, a pile of perfectly good, though unlit, candles beside him with a very dark kitchen in need of brightening only a few steps away.

He ran both hands through his hair once more, keeping his head fully bent down for several breaths. He could do this. He would stay levelheaded and unattached. Nothing was decided between Fezzi and Miss Smith, of that he was certain. Which meant nothing was decided between Fezzi and Belle, either.

He was the odd man out. As such, he would respect the wishes of those also staying in Easthill Manor. Which meant he would have to keep his distance from Belle. The thought alone caused him no small amount of pain.

CHAPTER TWELVE

Belle watched the two candles flicker atop the kitchen table. A barely lit room always felt so magical to her. And here it was St. Nicolas Day, one of the most magical times of the year. Now that she'd had a moment to collect herself, a bit of peace had entered her heart.

All was not lost. Fezzi clearly had not spoken for Miss Smith yet; that meant she still had time to convince him otherwise. She'd managed to speak with him one-on-one a couple of days ago as their paths had crossed just before breakfast, and he had seemed pleased with her company. Perhaps if she were a bit more like other women, he would notice her more? Harriet was quite outspoken, and she always had a bevy of gentlemen vying for her attention. Miss Smith was another example of the same. Belle had always known herself to be of a quiet nature; it was very possible she wasn't the sort of woman Fezzi wanted nor the kind of woman who deserved a title and respect.

The knock of boots against the floor brought her gaze up. After staring at the candles for so long, all she could make out was the general outline of a person walking into the kitchen.

Belle sat up straighter; if it was Fezzi, she would begin right now. She would endeavor, yet again, to make a place for herself in the conversation. She would show him that she did deserve to be among the *haut ton*.

"Are you the beautiful lady who requested more candles?" James's teasing tone reached her.

Belle smiled and stood. "Good; you found some."

He made his way over to the table and held out his hands, offering her the long, tapered candles.

"Where are Fezzi and Miss Smith?" she asked, slipping a candle out from between his fingers.

"Still looking for candles, I suppose. Fezzi and I parted as soon as we left the kitchen."

Belle placed the wick inside the flickering fire of another. It caught quickly, and Belle held it upright. "We'll for sure have plenty of light, then." She glanced about. "Oh dear, I don't suppose you brought a half dozen candle holders with you?"

"Sorry. I only have two hands."

Here she'd been close to tears only minutes ago, and now she was suddenly in the mood to tease. How did James do that? He was truly a very dear friend. "Well, since it is your fault that we are sadly lacking in candle holders, *you* shall have to hold this one while I search out something to place it in."

He held up the stack of tapered candles still between his palms. "As you may recall, I only have two hands."

"I won't let you cry off as easily as that." Belle placed a hand on her hip in a show of great determination. "If you don't have a hand free, then I may insist you carry it in your mouth."

She'd expected him to laugh, perhaps snap her a witty rejoinder. Instead, his gaze dropped to her lips then came back up with a jolt. He turned sharply away from her, opening his hands and practically pouring the candles all over the kitchen table.

"I'll find something," he muttered, turning his back toward her and hurrying off.

Belle reached a hand out, stopping two candles from rolling toward the table edge. Once they were secure once more, she looked back toward where James had disappeared into the shadows along the far wall. What had she done wrong? Perhaps her attempt at levity had not been so very clever, after all.

He'd always laughed at her jokes in the past. Was he, too, feeling the late hour? It was very likely he was anxious to have this Buche de Noel baked and done.

She should probably be more careful of what slipped out of her mouth in the future. If not even James found her tease about him holding a candle in his mouth humorous, then Fezzi certainly wouldn't have. *Always a lady.* That's what Mother had taught her. Ladies of high breeding didn't speak of such ridiculous things.

James stalked back over to her. She turned his direction, smiling, hoping to smooth over her clumsy misstep. But he didn't look her way.

"No candle holders. But perhaps we could make these work." He held up two tin bowls, tall while not being overly wide. He placed them on the table, then picked up a couple of candles and placed them inside. With their bases near the center of the bowls and their wicked ends resting over the brim, they seemed quite odd, yet functional. Belle reached out with the lit candle in her hand and spread its flame to each of the bowled candles. The room grew steadily brighter. It wasn't as good as a grand chandelier, or a large hearth fire, but there was enough to cook by now.

"They look like little candle wreaths," Belle said. "Excellent notion." She bumped her shoulder into his gently.

James rocked back. "I best see to finding the flour." Once more, he slipped into the dark corner of the room.

Where was the James who smiled with her? Why was it every time he grew overly worried she couldn't help but miss his usual lightheartedness? Though, tonight he didn't seem worried, exactly. There was something else bothering him. But she hadn't the faintest idea what it might be.

Belle rearranged a couple of the candles resting inside one of the bowls. By pushing one candle one direction, and another a different way, she got them to spread their light more evenly around the table. The bowl was better balanced as well; it would be awful if a bowl tipped over and scorched the table.

A grunting came from the direction James had gone.

Belle made sure all the lit candles were safe and then started after him. "James?" she called.

He only grunted a couple more times. It was like he was trying to lift something heavy or pull very hard on something unwilling to give.

She could easily imagine a large flour sack being very hard to move. Drawing nearer to the corner, she slowly made out the form of James, hands well above his head, tugging on a large sack.

Belle pursed her lips. "That can't possibly be the sack the cook uses daily." James was certainly taller than the cook and even he was struggling to reach it.

He gave it another tug, but the sack refused to move more than an inch. "It's the only one"—another grunt, another fruitless tug—"I could find."

With one more growl, James pulled on the sack. It tipped slightly to the side and split open. A large wave of flour dropped to the floor, covering James in the process.

Belle placed a hand against her mouth, trying to stifle her laughter. The flour billowed around James like an ethereal fog come to take him on a midnight journey.

He coughed while placing his hands atop his knees and bending over slightly. The flour floating about him settled.

James shook his head, kicking up the calming flour all over again.

Belle hurried to him. The small mounds of flour crunched like snow beneath her slippers as she drew near.

"Dear me," she said, brushing off his shoulders and arms. "I'm afraid that flour must be stuck on something."

"Truly?" he said, standing straight once more. "I was rather wondering if a ghost hadn't come and pushed it over on me."

She laughed softly, continuing to brush at his clothes. There was ever so much flour on him. "Why is it that I seem to be forever finding you covered in something or another? First dust, then snow, and now flour." His head was covered as well. Going up on tiptoes, Belle combed her fingers through his hair hoping to dislodge most of the white.

James's breath hitched.

Belle's gaze dropped to his face. He stood oh so very still. Her skin pricked with awareness of how close they stood to one another, of her fingers entwined in his hair, of his broad shoulders.

And his eyes. No one had ever looked at her quite like that. Though James and Fezzi looked a lot alike, their eyes were vastly different. Fezzi's were brown, and that was all.

But James's eyes were blue and expressive. They swirled with concern when he was worrying for Lady Wilkins. They sparked when jesting or throwing snowballs. They were deep and dark when comforting her.

Though he looked at her most intently, in the near-black of the corner, she could hardly tell what pooled inside them now.

His arm came up and wrapped around her waist. The touch sent heat skittering across her back. With so little light she could have been mistaken, but Belle thought she saw his gaze drop to her lips. An enticing pulse seemed to tug her toward him. She leaned ever so slightly closer, resting her hand against his chest.

Voices came from near the kitchen door. As one, Belle and James pulled apart. Fezzi and Miss Smith walked in that very moment, each with a three-candle candelabra in either hand.

"Hilli-ho," Fezzi called out, "anyone still in here?"

"We've found more than enough light," Miss Smith said cheerfully, placing her lights on the table.

Belle's face felt warm. Thank goodness the room, especially the corner she and James stood in, was so dark.

Fezzi placed his candles near Miss Smith's. "James, did you place these candles in the bowls?"

"How very peculiar," Miss Smith added.

"Yes, well, if you knew James as well as I do—" Fezzi turned then, facing them more fully. "Gads," he said, eying James, a smile growing across his face. "What did Belle do to you?" he joked.

Belle quickly drew herself up and walked back toward the table. "Oh no, he created this mess all on his own." She needed to shake off whatever it was that had just happened. Ignoring the tingles of lingering heat atop her skin, Belle stood across the kitchen table from Miss Smith. "Where do we start?"

CHAPTER THIRTEEN

The next morning dawned. Belle found herself lying in bed rather later than usual, the sunlight pouring into the room despite the curtains being drawn.

She'd started last night feeling downcast, and yet, by the time she'd retired to bed, she'd felt decidedly more lighthearted. Every time she thought of James, covered from head to toe in flour, she wanted to laugh all over again.

Rolling out of bed, she quickly dressed and joined the rest of the house in the breakfast room. Apparently, she wasn't the only one who'd slept in a bit late. James hadn't even come down yet, it seemed.

"How is your head this morning?" Belle asked as she sat down next to Lady Wilkins. The dear woman had complained of a small ache just as Belle, James, Fezzi, and Miss Smith had finished their baking.

"Much better; thank you for asking." Lady Wilkins sipped a bit of drinking chocolate. "You seem rather radiant this morning, dear."

Belle felt radiant which was most unusual for her. "I

suppose it is the Christmas magic working its charm, but I feel quite as though all is right in the world."

Lady Wilkins smiled. "I am glad to hear it. Were you up very late after we all retired?"

Belle shook her head. "I chose to go straight to bed, instead of staying up to sew." She had been feeling so lighthearted by the night's end, she had considered pulling out her puppets and working on them some more. In the end, she'd simply lain in bed, laughing at the memories the night had made. Still, she had spent far less time on her puppets this year than she usually did.

Lady Wilkins set her cup down. "Are your puppets nearly done then?"

"Puppets?" Miss Smith broke into the conversation. "Great Jehoshaphat, please tell me you don't have any of those creepy things in your room, Miss Young."

Fezzi leaned across the table, closer to Miss Smith. "For years now, Belle has put on a small performance every Twelfth Night for the children of servants and tenants. It's a silly tradition I suppose, but she insists upon it all the same."

He said it with a smile, his tone not exactly condescending, yet a tug of disappointment made Belle want to shrink down in her chair. She'd known he didn't exactly applaud her little performance, but she hadn't thought he saw it so far beneath himself.

Miss Smith only giggled, as though she, too, believed Belle's puppets were the act of a child. As Belle watched Fezzi and Miss Smith lean in and whisper something brief, the drinking chocolate on Belle's tongue grew bitter and she tried, unsuccessfully, to swallow it quickly. With any luck, she could drown the jealousy growing in her stomach.

Miss Smith quickly cast aside the topic of Belle and her puppets and started a new one. "There are just so many things we could choose to do today. I hardly know where to begin."

"You are a guest here," Fezzi replied. "Whatever you choose, we will make happen."

Belle drew herself up—she had promised herself to be more forward, had she not? No matter what everyone thought of her puppets, she wasn't going to be shoved aside any longer. "Fezzi and I always go ice skating on the day after St. Nicolas."

Miss Smith looked at her, clearly surprised, but she quickly brushed off the expression in favor of one of pure delight. "First sledding and now ice skating? Oh, that sounds scrumptious!"

Not two hours later, they were all bundled up and quickly arranging themselves in two sleighs. The Smiths, including Sarah and Nancy, along with Lady Wilkins, took up one, while Miss Smith sat beside Belle in the second.

Fezzi pulled himself inside after handing both women up.

Belle's face dropped. "Where is James?" Surely they wouldn't go without him.

Fezzi shrugged. "He claims disinterest in ice skating today."

How odd. Was he, perhaps, hoping to use the time to search for the all-important letter regarding Lady Wilkins? With everyone away, it would avail him time to search more public rooms in the manor.

Should she offer to stay and help?

Fezzi pounded on the side of the sleigh and the driver started them forward. Of course, there was no guarantee that *was* what James planned to do. It was every bit as likely that he simply didn't care for ice skating. Or that he desired some quiet time to himself after many days in constant company. Slowly, Easthill Manor slipped from view.

Lips still pursed, Belle turned back and faced the others in the sleigh. The ride was taken up with Miss Smith talking and Fezzi readily agreeing with her. It was rather odd, but Belle had remembered Fezzi being a bit more engaging in previous years.

Then again, with Miss Smith's rapid conversation, she supposed anyone would appear boring in contrast.

The lake came into view along Belle's right. She looked out over it. So many memories filled this small part of the woods. She and Fezzi had been coming here for years, as had most of Dunwell. Though, that final time, three years ago, had been quite the most fun. The memories rushed over her as the sleigh stopped and Fezzi handed them out.

Belle had almost not joined Fezzi and James that day. She had been feeling quite self-conscious of wanting to appear ladylike and grown-up and hadn't been at all sure she could keep her balance on the ice. But in the end, both gentlemen had insisted she come. She could particularly remember the way James had taken hold of her hand and promised not to laugh any of the times she fell. It had sounded to her like a challenge she couldn't pass up.

"This is quite picturesque, is it not, Miss Young?" Miss Smith asked, linking her arm through Belle's. "I do have to admit, though, that I have gone skating no more than three times in my entire life. I don't know if I shall be able to stay upright at all. It looks rather painful to fall, but then I guess that's all the more motivation to apply oneself to staying upright."

One of the footmen brought the metal blades over and helped to secure them to the bottom of Belle's boots. As he moved to help Miss Smith, Belle took the three steps toward the frozen lake with care. The trickiest step was often the first one when a person left the snow behind and began gliding across the ice.

Three years ago, Belle had returned home with Fezzi and James, pleased to report to Lady Wilkins that she hadn't fallen once, while James had fallen at least four times. She was pretty sure he'd fallen more than that but had stood before she'd caught him in the act.

With a gentle kick, Belle began to slide down the lake. She inhaled deeply, letting the sounds of other skaters wash over her. How was it that cold had a smell? It was ever so hard to explain and yet quite easy to distinguish. Once one had 'smelled' cold, there was no denying it did indeed carry its own scent. Belle had practiced ice skating much these past few years. Partially so she never had to feel self-conscious again when invited to go ice skating. Partially because it was an excellent excuse for getting out of the house and away from her family. And partially so she could beat James if ever the opportunity availed itself.

A shriek carried over the ice. Belle turned around and looked back the way she'd come. Miss Smith clutched tightly to Fezzi as her feet slipped every which direction. Belle skated over to them, taking Miss Smith's arm on the side opposite of Fezzi.

"I warned you both," Miss Smith said, laughing even as she almost fell and took them both down with her.

Belle's heart went out to her—she herself had felt awkward on the ice many times as a youth. Truth was, Belle couldn't help but admire Miss Smith's fortitude and willingness to try something new. If she'd met the young American woman in any other circumstances, Belle felt certain they could have become the best of friends.

"Don't watch your feet," Fezzi instructed in a calm, even tone. "Keep them closer together...that's it. Careful, now."

Belle's stomach churned; he'd spoken to her that way once. Fezzi had first brought her out on the ice when she was but ten. He had taken both her hands in his and said very nearly the same words he spoke to Miss Smith now.

They continued on and within a few minutes, Miss Smith was making a marked improvement. Belle found, as she let go, that she was no longer needed to keep anyone upright.

Fezzi and Miss Smith skated on past her, neither one

commenting on her sudden disappearance. An ache began in her chest. She very slowly slid across the ice, trailing well behind them, a few other couples passing her by as well. Eventually, she spotted a log lying near the edge of the pond. She skated up to it and placed a hand on it, testing its strength. Confident it would hold her, she sat, alone, well away from all others.

Fezzi and Miss Smith picked up speed; the squeal of her laughter could be heard from across the pond as they made a turn.

For the first time today, Belle felt the cold. It chaffed her nose and cheeks. If this was how Lady Wilkins felt every time she stepped outside during winter, it was no wonder the woman rarely left the house. Fezzi and Miss Smith came closer to Belle. If they looked up and waved her toward them, she would have no logical reason to remain seated. Fezzi knew she very much enjoyed skating; it was only *today* she wasn't having any fun.

Fezzi and Miss Smith passed by, not so much as glancing her way. Belle wrapped her arms tighter around her.

She should just get up and skate.

What did it matter if Miss Smith needed Fezzi's attention just now? He wouldn't forget her completely—surely not.

What did it matter if she weren't so elegant or lovely or well-poised? Fezzi had never cared overly for such things —had he?

"Who is that with Lord Wilkins?" An elderly woman's voice sounded behind Belle.

"Oh. I don't know," another deep-voiced woman answered. "You don't suppose it's that same woman he used to bring here every year? What was her name?"

The first woman made a noncommittal guffaw. "Miss something-or-other. But surely he has moved on from *her*."

"No doubt," the second replied. "Such a mousy little thing, she was."

The two women moved around the pond and away from Belle. Their words hurt far more than she cared to admit. Where were Fezzi and Miss Smith? No doubt, attaching herself to them, unneeded though she was, would certainly be better than this.

Setting her feet squarely on the ice, she pushed to a stand and gently made her way in a large circle around the ice. She spotted them easily enough; many individuals were on the ice, but not so many as to hide Fezzi and Miss Smith. Fezzi's arm was still around Miss Smith though she appeared quite at her ease already.

Belle had originally intended to join them once more, but as she drew near she simply couldn't find it within her to foist herself upon them.

She had been doing just that for years now—foisting herself upon Fezzi, wanted or not. Belle tilted her feet slightly to the side and skated around them in a wide arc.

But she *had* been wanted. Fezzi had promised. Surely she hadn't misremembered the entire conversation.

Fear tightened in her midsection. If Fezzi did not come up to scratch, what would she do?

When she'd spoken up that morning and suggested ice skating, she hadn't imagined it would turn out like *this*.

When Belle noticed Miss Smith making her way back toward the edge of the ice, she took her opportunity and skated between couples and over to Fezzi.

"Don't mind me," Miss Smith said. "You keep right on skating. I only need to sit for a moment."

"We can return to the house if that's what you wish," Fezzi immediately replied.

"Nonsense." Miss Smith sat atop an obliging stump. "I'm fine right here."

Belle reached them and placed a hand on Fezzi's arm. "Suppose we take a turn or two," she said, "and then we can see Miss Smith back to Easthill Manor."

Miss Smith nodded. "That sounds just right."

Fezzi seemed torn, his gaze jumping between Belle and Miss Smith. "Are you quite sure?"

"Yes," Miss Smith said, motioning for one of the manservants to help her remove the blades from her boots. "Quite sure."

Fezzi nodded, pushing away from the edge of the ice. Belle fell into easy stride with him. Still, he glanced back at Miss Smith frequently.

Belle drew her lower lip in between her teeth; this was her chance, her opportunity to remind Fezzi that she had been here before Miss Smith.

Gracious, when she thought in those terms, she felt positively selfish. Belle shook her head. She couldn't lose her nerve now, because she couldn't live with Aunt Agnes forever and she couldn't be "that little mousy thing" to all and sundry. She deserved love and a home too, didn't she?

"Are you quite all right?" Fezzi asked.

"Yes, of course," she said quickly. Here she was, wasting her one chance by woolgathering. "I was only thinking of how much fun we used to have every winter."

Fezzi chuckled softly. "Like the year we climbed the trees near the main road and lobbed snowballs at passing carriages."

"Or the year we stole your father's favorite top hat and greatcoat for our snowman," Belle added.

"Or the year," Fezzi continued, growing excited, "that we shined all the coffee cups with smelly fish oil."

"Or the year we put old cheese in the mistletoe and garland downstairs, and every time your tutor tried to kiss—"

"Tried to kiss Eliza's abigail—"

"—the smell was too overwhelming." Belle laughed and Fezzi joined in.

He shook his head. "We have had many an adventure, have we not?"

Too many for either of them to simply walk away from the other. But perhaps it was only *she* who thought so. "Or that one year," Belle clung tightly to whatever courage she could muster, "that you found me crying during the Twelfth Night ball." It had been the year before he left—the moment he'd promised to take her away from Wilmington Bury for good.

Fezzi's smile slipped. He coughed uncomfortably and looked away. "Many adventures, to be sure." He drew himself back up. "Shall we see to returning home?" He pushed off, harder than before and Belle had to scramble to keep up.

They spoke not a word as they skated around the rest of the lake, which was growing more crowded by the minute, and back over to Miss Smith. Once their brief, albeit diverting, conversation had met an untimely end, all of Belle's courage slipped away. She had neither the words nor the audacity to push further.

In only a few minutes, they were all headed back toward the sleigh and then back to Easthill Manor.

Belle leaned into her seat, emotionally exhausted and still no closer to securing a future for herself.

CHAPTER FOURTEEN

James tried to ignore the pounding in his head as he rested it back against the squabs as the conveyance he had borrowed from Fezzi's carriage house rolled through Dunwell. His headache was due, no doubt, to his deuced lack of sleep last night.

Oh no, he created this mess all on his own.

That's what Belle had said. She hadn't known how accurate she'd been. Not only in terms of the flour, which he'd foolishly pulled down on himself in a feverish attempt to distract himself from how stunning she was in candlelight, but in terms of the mess brooding inside him as well.

Blast, but he'd nearly kissed her. She'd stood so very close to him, and he couldn't seem to force his feet to move away no matter how his head had insisted it was the best course of action. May the heavens be his witness, he had tried; but his traitorous feet had simply refused to obey. Then, as if her close proximity and the candlelight hadn't been enough, she'd run her fingers through his hair. The world had melted away. For a brief moment, there had been no letter to find, no Fezzi to be concerned over, no one and nothing else. Only him and Belle and candlelight.

Lud, but he was grateful Fezzi and Miss Smith had come in when they had. A moment later and he would have been caught in the act of kissing a woman whom he respected and admired, and who most assuredly did *not* want to be kissed. At least not by him. The last thing he wanted was to ruin the friendship between them.

The carriage rolled to a stop and a footman opened the door for him. James stepped out. The cold winter air was not too frigid today, but he suspected that Mr. Scrooge's place of business was icy inside, no matter the weather.

He hurried up to the door and once more cracked the knocker against the metal plate.

Mr. Cratchit opened the door with a well-worn smile, just like before. "Mr. Radcliff, come in, come in. So glad you were able to make it today."

James stepped inside; sure enough, the space somehow managed to feel even colder than the open air outside. "I appreciated the missive you sent me." James glanced around, but Mr. Scrooge was nowhere to be seen.

Mr. Cratchit only shook the compliment off. "Never you mind that. I only wish I could have persuaded Mr. Scrooge to introduce you to Mr. Jacob without all this twisting about." The elderly man leaned in closer, as though he intended to whisper, yet his voice was no quieter than before. "I tried; for your sake, I truly did. But there was nothing for it. As it stands, Mr. Jacob has agreed to happen by in a few minutes. If you are meeting with Mr. Scrooge at that time, well, he very well can't refuse you, can he?"

James was growing to like this cheerful old man. He hadn't been sure what to think that morning when he'd received the missive from Mr. Cratchit, but now he was quite glad he'd excused himself from the ice-skating trip and come here instead. "I think it an excellent notion. Though, might I ask why Mr. Scrooge is so opposed to providing an introduction?"

"Oh, that is a bit of a story." Mr. Cratchit's voice wobbled as he spoke. "I'll just say that Mr. Jacob decided one day that he no longer wanted to be the man he'd been. He changed his name after that, changed his whole life, too. I think, in a lot of ways, Mr. Scrooge feels Mr. Jacob *did* die. I—"

Steps down the hallway silenced Mr. Cratchit. James looked past the old man and saw Mr. Scrooge coming their way.

"Mr. Radcliff," he said, his voice as cold as his place of business. "We do not have a meeting scheduled for today—or any day."

"I understand that," James said, following him into the same room where they'd spoken before.

Mr. Cratchit followed in quietly as well, slipping back behind his own desk.

"Well, then?" Mr. Scrooge pressed.

Mr. Cratchit had said Mr. Jacob—or whatever his name was now—would be along any minute. He only needed to drag the conversation out for a bit. Hopefully.

"I wanted to discuss something with you." What that thing was, he needed to think up fast. James sat in the same wooden chair he'd taken before, despite Mr. Scrooge not offering it.

With a muttered grumble, Mr. Scrooge also took his seat behind the large desk.

"I was wondering," James tried, "if you had found any more information regarding Mr. Thrup?" That seemed as good a topic as any.

"If I had, I would have written," Mr. Scrooge huffed.

"Yes, I had hoped you would. But I wanted to come and check, all the same."

"Very well," Mr. Scrooge stood. "If that is all."

James shifted about in his chair; he couldn't leave just yet.

He opened his mouth, but nothing come to mind. He shifted again. There had to be something he could bring up, something—

A knock sounded at the door.

James relaxed back into the hard chair. Mr. Scrooge's expression hardened, and he flicked a finger toward Mr. Cratchit, wordlessly ordering the elderly man to answer the door.

Mr. Cratchit's walk was slow. For the interim, James did little more than silently pray the newcomer was, indeed, Mr. Jacob.

He and Mr. Scrooge waited in silence as the front door was opened and voices carried into the room. Whoever had come was clearly a man and one with many years in his cap by the sound of it, though not nearly one so old as Mr. Cratchit.

Both men walked into the room, and James found he had to look quite far up. Mr. Jacob was a very tall man, apparently. Thin, too. His face and nose were both long, and though his hair was white, he stood with a confident bearing. His clothing, though, is what most caught James's eye. The robes made Mr. Jacob's new profession quite clear—the man had chosen the church.

"Greetings of the season," he said, jovially.

"How now!" came Mr. Scrooge's caustic voice. "What do you want?"

"Much," Mr. Jacob said, his voice as smooth as Mr. Scrooge's was rough. "But, first, perhaps you ought to introduce me?" he asked, turning slightly toward James.

"Bah," Mr. Scrooge said under his breath. He flicked a hand toward James. "This is Mr. Radcliff."

James stood and bowed. "It is an honor, sir," he said, and then, since Mr. Scrooge seemed to have finished the introductions only halfway through, James added, "And you are?"

"Ask me who I *was*."

"I don't mean to sound presumptuous, sir, but I would have to guess that you *were* Mr. Jacob, Mr. Scrooge's partner of many years."

The tall man inclined his head. "That is correct, though that life is quite behind me now."

Mr. Scrooge sat heavily behind his desk and dropped his head, studying the ledger before him. He appeared quite determined to ignore the conversation happening directly over his head. Not that it bothered James very much; Mr. Scrooge was by no means an easy man to converse with.

Mr. Cratchit spoke up. "Since you're here, Mr. Radcliff had a question regarding a loan you made nearly thirty years ago."

"Is that so?" Mr. Jacob said. James still didn't know what the man went by currently so had to think of him thusly; but the task at hand was far more important than the tall vicar's name.

"Yes, a man by the name of Mr. Thrup. Do you remember him?"

Mr. Jacob pressed his lips into a tight line as his brow creased in thought. "The name does not bring to mind..." His eyes grew wide. "Actually, yes. Yes, I do believe I remember him. I believe," he added slowly, "the man had a particular tie to the town. A...friendship, if you will."

Apparently James was not the only one who knew the truth. "To one, Lady Wilkins."

"The very one."

James could not like learning that yet another individual held the information which could destroy Fezzi. But at least he knew for sure Mr. Jacob spoke of the correct Mr. Thrup. "I need to find Mr. Thrup. Have you any knowledge of where he might be now?"

"Yes, actually," Mr. Jacob said. "I know exactly where he is."

James's pulse quickened. Mr. Thrup was as good as found. Now, James only needed to decide on the best approach—the best words to instill in Mr. Thrup the necessity of keeping his secret to himself.

Mr. Jacob continued. "He rests in the church graveyard, third row from the back, nearest the willow tree."

Oh. The anticipation of before seemed to collapse in on itself.

"He passed on nearly fifteen years ago."

Gads, that changed things. James placed a hand against his forehead but couldn't seem to find the right words to say. To speak with joy about another man's demise would be unseemly. But now there was no need to worry the man would try to ruin Fezzi. It was probably wicked, but James couldn't help but feel relief at the news.

That left only the letter to be found and dealt with. For the first time since Mrs. Gaight had whispered her dreadful secret, James felt optimistic. He could handle a letter, surely. Once that was seen to, Fezzi would be safe, secure in his earldom forever.

James looked up and found Mr. Jacob speaking his farewells and making his way toward the door.

"Thank you for your time, Mr. Scrooge," James spoke quickly, then turned toward the tall vicar. "I am on my way out as well."

Mr. Jacob slowed his step so that James could catch up and they passed outside one right behind the other.

"I hope my information was not too distressing," he said.

James shook his head; the news was *far* from distressing. "Not at all. Though I do not relish in the death of any man, it is beneficial information to have, all the same."

"I have not seen you in the pew with Lord Wilkins or his mother and their other guests."

James slowed his step. "You know I'm staying at Easthill Manor?"

The man smiled a very gentle, vicary smile. Apparently, when the man had changed professions, he'd chosen a well-fitting one.

"I try to keep a close eye on the flock I am responsible for."

"Even old misers like Mr. Scrooge?" James had meant it as a sort of joke.

Instead, Mr. Jacob's expression grew solemn. "I hired him right out of school. Took him on and mentored him. In many ways, I am responsible for the man he has become." Mr. Jacob turned back toward the place of business now several buildings behind them. "Perhaps, if I am so lucky, one of these days I shall see even the likes of him changed."

That would require a Christmas miracle—though James felt it best to keep such an observation to himself. "I understand, sir, that you are no longer Mr. Jacob."

The tall man slowly shook his head, his gaze still on the building they'd left. "The knowledge of all I'd done finally weighed too heavily on me to continue. So I took my mother's maiden name and entered the church."

"You seem to have a gift for lightening the load of those around you," James said. "You certainly have done as much for me."

The vicar's lips turned upward. "We must all give to those who mean the most to us. During this time of year, it is all the more important."

James found himself agreeing. He may not have been born an heir apparent, but he certainly had been blessed with many wonderful friends through the years. Not the least of which was Belle, who'd unknowingly helped him shoulder his own weight these past weeks. Perhaps it was time he give something to her. She'd mentioned a while back that she frequently ran low on thread while sewing her puppets. If he hurried, he would have just enough time to pick some up before returning to Easthill Manor.

Excited over what he'd learned regarding Mr. Thrup, and eager to find Belle the perfect gift, James stretched out his hand. "Well, I thank you, sir. If you will excuse me, I believe I have another stop to make."

Mr. Jacob shook his hand. "It is always a pleasure to be of service. I do hope to see you in the future." He began to walk away.

James watched him, suddenly hesitant to let him go. He couldn't help but feel intrigued by a man who was so obviously different from Mr. Scrooge, yet who, supposedly, had once been so much the same. "And if we should meet," James called after him, "what shall I call you?"

The vicar only turned halfway around, speaking over his shoulder. "I am Mr. Marley."

CHAPTER FIFTEEN

After leaving Mr. Scrooge and Mr. Marley that afternoon, James had had a startling realization—one that left him both agitated and enlivened.

Now that there was no threat from Mr. Thrup, James could speak openly to Fezzi about both Miss Smith and Belle. The memory of Belle in his arms had only grown all the more heady, and he could hardly think of anything else. Of course, he had to speak with Fezzi before...before what, he couldn't say. But he knew he needed to speak with Fezzi *before*.

It was still unclear to James exactly what the understanding between Fezzi and Belle was. Had anything been said? If so, what and when? Moreover, what did it all mean now? If Fezzi had come to his senses and wished to pursue Belle, James would not stand in the way. However, if Fezzi was more taken with Miss Smith, that would leave Belle available. If that were the case, well...James grew nervous and anxious every time he thought of it.

"Really, Mr. Radcliff," Miss Smith said from across the music room. "You are in such bad spirits today. You should be smiling. It is Christmas time after all, and we shall soon be spirited away to a grand ball."

James tried to smile and nod his agreement, but his face didn't follow through on its part of the deception very well. James grunted and reclined further into the grand wingback.

"Well," Miss Smith continued, pacing across the room and toward the door which led to the corridor beyond, "I am sure *I* am looking forward to this evening's events. I must confess to being quite excited at meeting more of Fezzi's friends. If his other associates are anywhere near as congenial as you and Miss Young, I shall return to America quite green with jealousy, I'm sure."

"Congenial?" James said. "I thought you just accused me of being in bad spirits?"

She laughed. "You are *tonight*. But even put out as you are, you are far nicer than many a gentleman I've met while in one of their good moods. Miss Young," she suddenly called out the door. "Is that what you're wearing tonight?"

James placed his feet firmly on the floor and his elbows against his legs. He stared at the floor. If he kept his gaze on the floor he wouldn't see her. And if he didn't see her, there was far less of a chance that he'd do something he'd regret. He truly needed to speak with Fezzi. Things needed to be settled and agreed upon between him and Belle before James showed her all she'd begun to mean to him. Else wise, he'd do nothing but drive her away, he was sure.

Tonight, he would keep his distance. Tonight, he wouldn't allow himself to get anywhere *near* making a momentous blunder. If it meant not so much as looking at or speaking with Belle, he would do it.

He thought he heard Belle answer in the affirmative, but Miss Smith's voice carried over it. "You look quite ravishing. I am certain you shall turn more heads tonight than any other lady in the room."

Though he couldn't make out her words specifically, James knew the cadence of Belle's voice well enough to understand that she'd said, "Thank you." Devil take him, a man should not know the subtle intonations of the voice belonging to a woman who was quite set on another. Did Belle still prefer Fezzi to all others? Or had she begun to have feelings for him, too?

No matter what she felt, it was clear from her actions that she still had her cap set at Fezzi. The frustration from before soured his stomach once again. No matter Mr. Thrup was no longer an issue, Belle still wanted Fezzi, not James, and he didn't know if such would ever change.

Perhaps he should cry off and head to bed early. With Belle at the ball and himself locked securely in his bedchamber, at least he wouldn't risk losing what had quickly become a most important friendship.

"Come, Mr. Radcliff."

Though James didn't look up, he heard Miss Smith and Belle's footsteps draw near.

"Do you not think Belle will find her dance card full within thirty minutes of us arriving?"

He reminded himself that he'd decided *not* to look over at Belle tonight, lest it lead to trouble. Still, the hem of her dress was quite a lovely shade of primrose yellow. How it was layered across her waist emphasized her slenderness and somehow made his hands ache to hold her. The gentle trim of lavender, which wove over her stomach and down the skirt, probably also looked quite elegant against the turn of her neck.

He finally glanced up. Oh, *it did*. Her hair looked quite lovely, too. Most of it was curled atop her head with small, white flowers woven in, while a few ringlets had been left dangling. Her eyes, though, were the part of her that always drew him in.

James blinked; blast, but he'd begun to stare. He stood abruptly. "Pardon me, but I am not up to attending tonight after all." He hadn't been able to keep to his objective for a full five minutes. Going would only spell disaster.

Miss Smith tsked. "You are being unforgivably rude," she told James then turned toward Belle. "He has been in poor spirits ever since I came down. You won't be downcast for his lack of manners, will you? Regardless of what Mr. Radcliff thinks, you are a vision."

Belle watched him, her soft eyes seeming to search out what he truly thought.

If only he could tell her.

Miss Smith had the right of it; of that there was no doubt. Belle was a vision. James wholeheartedly agreed. It was the very reason he couldn't attend tonight. A solid night away from Belle and her bewitching smile, and perhaps he could set his heart aright once more.

"Please excuse me," he said, making to walk around the two women.

"You cannot be serious," Miss Smith called after him. "Christmas time happens but once a year. I'm sure it would be bad luck for you not to attend tonight."

James stopped near the door. Turning back toward Miss Smith, he kept his eyes decidedly away from Belle. "I beg your pardon, but I'm afraid I must insist. Fezzi will escort you both, and I pray you all have a wonderful time."

"Are you sure you won't come?" Belle asked. Her soft voice was a sharp contrast to Miss Smith's. "Suppose you came for a dance or two, and then if you were still of a mind to retire early, you could leave then?"

"Oh, yes." Miss Smith picked up the suggestion. "There's a very good chance that once you start dancing, you won't wish to stop. It may be that you are only a bit bedraggled from a long week. A bit of a social whirl is all you need to set you right again."

"We promise not to stay long if you don't wish it," Belle added.

James felt his resolve sway. It would be best for all if he didn't join them, yet Belle's look led him to believe she truly wished him to be there. Plus, the thought of dancing with her was far more alluring than he cared to admit.

Fezzi walked in, blowing out a loud breath. "We won't be staying long at all, it seems."

All eyes turned toward him. Though he was dressed quite in the first stare of fashion, the corners of his mouth hung low on one side. "My mother's headache of last night has returned. Only tonight it is far more violent. She will not be attending with us." He tapped his thigh, clearly distressed. "If it is all right with you all,"—though he addressed everyone, James felt he was truly only speaking to Miss Smith—"I feel I should stay as well."

Miss Smith hurried to his side, slipping her arm around his.

"Do you think the headache truly so bad?" Belle asked, sincere concern in her voice.

James was tempted to glance her way; he knew the way her brows would draw together, and she would most likely fret over her bottom lip. He stopped himself just in time.

"I don't know," Fezzi said at length. "She claims it is not much, but, lately..."

Belle slowly walked over to Fezzi, facing him directly. "She has grown old while you were away."

Fezzi's face fell. "I can see that now. What an ungrateful son I've been, deserting her for three years."

Miss Smith squeezed his arm. "I'm certain your mother would not want you blaming yourself."

James agreed with her, and Belle said so as well.

Fezzi, his expression still heavy, turned to James. "I'm afraid it's up to you to escort these lovely women to the Christmas ball tonight."

"No." Miss Smith spoke up before James could even open his mouth. "Mr. Radcliff had determined not to attend either. He is far too melancholy for anything as gay as a ball."

"Is this true?" Fezzi asked.

James nodded, but, yet again, was not permitted enough time to actually speak.

"I know just the thing," Miss Smith said, excitedly. "We shall have our own little Christmas ball, here. Just the four of us."

What? That would not do at all. James's gaze jumped to Belle; she was not looking at him, but she seemed every bit as surprised by the notion as he felt.

"That way," Miss Smith continued, "you can stay near your sweet mother in case she has need of you, Mr. Radcliff is in no danger of being cheered up, and Miss Young and I can still show off our lovely gowns to two of the most handsome men in all England."

Fezzi shook his head slowly. "I would hate to deprive you of an evening I know you were quite looking forward to."

"Nonsense," Miss Smith pressed. "It is decided. We shall have our own ball."

Just the four of them? It would be imminently harder to avoid Belle with no crush of people to hide behind. "What of your parents, and sister?" he asked. "Would they not care to join us?"

"On hearing my mother wished to retire early," Fezzi said, "Mr. and Mrs. Smith decided to do the same."

Miss Smith finished for him. "And Sarah and Nancy are already in the nursery, reading for the night." She tugged on Fezzi's arm, leading him further into the room. "Come now, we shall begin immediately. You shall all see, four is the perfect number for a ball."

Miss Smith led them all toward the pianoforte, which sat quite stately near a far corner. She sat at the bench, directing everyone with a flick of her hand. "Miss Young and I will take turns playing music, while the other one of us dances. I am sorry for the gentlemen," she added with a feigned sigh of regret. "There appears to not be enough ladies in attendance tonight and one of you shall have to sit out every dance."

James shook his head, his tumultuous mood calming in spite of himself. "I still insist we should have invited your sisters. At least then Fezzi and I could both dance."

"Ah," Miss Smith countered, her fingers beginning the first strains of a Christmas carol, "but we could not have invited Sarah without Nancy, and then one of the *ladies* would have had to sit out for every song."

"Such would be regrettable," James agreed.

Miss Smith turned to the pianoforte in earnest, smiling as she played the opening slow chords to *Adeste Fideles*. She paused after only a couple of measures, her gaze jumping from James to Fezzi. "Well, don't stand there like dolts," she scolded. "One of you ask Miss Young to dance."

James immediately dropped his head, looking somewhere halfway between the pianoforte and the floor. Belle probably wasn't wishing for *him* to be the one to ask her.

"But," Fezzi said, "this isn't a song meant for dancing."

James could hear the hint of petulance in Miss Smith's voice. "Perhaps not, but it is almost the Holyday and I want a Christmas carol. Use your imagination."

"What of *Sir Roger de Coverley*?" Fezzi continued. "I love a lively country dance during the jolly holidays."

Miss Smith did not relent, however. "There is no talk of the holy baby in that song. It's not a Christmas carol without talk of the holy baby. Now, ask Miss Young to dance."

Still looking down, James saw only Fezzi's Hessians as he moved across the rug to where Belle stood.

"Would you do me the honor?" Fezzi asked her.

Belle curtsied and they began a most diverting display of trying to come up with dance steps to a song which was nothing like a cotillion, a reel, or a minuet. Fezzi and Belle had stepped on one another's feet several times, they'd had to pause repeatedly in order to debate the next "proper" step, and at one point Fezzi even accidentally backed into Miss Smith requiring her to stop playing completely as her hands were needed to brace herself lest she be knocked off the bench. By that point, they were all laughing.

After the song ended and among many chuckles and giggles, Belle took to the piano.

"I challenge you and James to dance any more gracefully," she said to Miss Smith. "You laugh now, but it's not nearly as easy as it looks."

"Oh," James countered, "it has to be easier than you and Fezzi made it look."

Belle shot him a scowl, belied by the smile she tried and failed to hide.

He bowed, Miss Smith curtsied, and Belle began to play *Bring a Torch, Jeanette, Isabella*. As it turned out, Belle had the right of it. Imagining up a new dance, while dancing with a partner who kept ordering him about and telling him how it *truly ought to be done* was most unsuccessful.

The song ended with Fezzi laughing so hard, James half wondered how he remained standing. Belle, too, was giggling to the point she could barely finish the song.

"Now," Miss Smith said, hurrying back toward the pianoforte. "Mr. Radcliff and Miss Young, it is your turn."

James's gaze flew to Belle. She smiled at him easily—quite as though she *hadn't* been thinking about his arms around her all day, quite as though she *hadn't* been imagining a shared kiss between them ever since last night, quite as though she *hadn't* realized the grave necessity of keeping their distance from one another. But he had. He'd done all that and more. They may be having a joyful "ball" now, but if he danced with Belle there was a very good chance he'd turn bacon-brained and do something foolish enough to ruin the night for everyone.

James opened his mouth, willing his mind to come up with something—*anything*—he might do instead of dance with Belle. "I've a grand idea"—he started speaking even as the plan formulated—"Belle and Fezzi should stand up together. Again."

Everyone looked at him, but it was Fezzi who spoke the question. "Why? What will you be doing?"

What could he be doing? There had to be something. "I shall be"—think—"getting us all Buche de Noel." Yes, that should work. "There was some left over from this morning. It's not a ball without refreshments." He took a couple of steps toward the door. "You two dance and I shall be back in time to claim my next dance with Miss Smith."

He could feel their stares trailing after him, but James left, nonetheless. It hadn't been precisely as elegant an exit as he'd hoped for, but it had been effective.

The kitchen was as dark tonight as it had been the previous evening. James had expected as much and so brought an already lit candle from the corridor with him. The chocolate cake, shaped like a log, was nothing new to James. But he had to admit that Miss Smith had not exaggerated the delicate flavor of her family's particular receipt. It was unequivocally delicious.

After taking the cake in one hand and a few forks with it, James turned and came face to face with the corner in which he had been doused in flour the night before. Seeing the spot sent a rush of heat through his limbs. Belle had stood so close to him. The feel of her fingers in his hair refused to leave.

James shook his head so hard he very nearly tossed the cake

onto the floor. Balancing it all once more, he strode from the kitchen. Distance, he reminded himself; he needed distance.

James reentered the room to find it different than when he'd left. Miss Smith still sat at the pianoforte, but Fezzi was not dancing with Belle. Instead, he sat on the bench with Miss Smith, their heads quite close together.

James sat the Buche de Noel atop a pier table between two of the tall, elegant windows. Where was Belle? No doubt, being left alone with Fezzi and Miss Smith in such an intimate nearness would have been quite uncomfortable for her. He looked over the entire room but didn't see her present. Neither Fezzi nor Miss Smith seemed to have noticed his return at all.

The door leading to the balcony outside was slightly ajar. Surely Belle wouldn't have ventured outside on such a cold night? He took long strides toward the door all the same. As James neared the door, he recognized Belle's slight frame silhouetted by moonlight. Softly falling snow danced around her. She had to be freezing. James paused. There had been a time when Lady Wilkins kept blankets inside the window seat, in case one grew cold while reading there. Did she still?

He turned away from the door, hurrying over to the window seat and pulling it up. The very same blankets of old were folded inside. He pulled out the biggest and made his way out the door.

Snow crunched beneath his boots. Belle didn't turn his way but kept her face toward the forest. James let the blanket open and then draped it over her shoulders. Being so near her, he could smell the hint of vanilla that always followed her. The way the moonlight played off her ringlets, it was all he could do not to reach out and wrap one around a finger.

With much effort, he pulled away, turning around and leaning back against the railing she held onto so that they could see each other easily even while they faced opposite directions.

"Tired of the ball already?" he asked, but the levity he hoped for seemed to fall flat.

Belle sighed, her shoulders slumping. James knew a moment of intense desire to reach out and hold her as he had before. But, no. He wouldn't, not tonight.

"Oh, James," she said, barely above a whisper. "What must you think of me?"

CHAPTER SIXTEEN

He was watching her closely. Belle felt James's gaze so intently, she could scarce take a breath.

"I hold you in nothing less than the highest esteem," James said.

His praise only made her all the more angry with herself. A true lady would not be trying to convince a gentleman who was in love with one woman to love her instead. "What a nitwit I've been."

James leaned forward, as if to reach for her, but pulled back at the last minute. "No, Belle, don't speak like that."

She shook her head, finding it necessary to blink a few times to keep the tears at bay. She was so tired of crying. "You cannot have been blind to the happenings...to my intentions..."

James's mouth tightened into a thin line. Though they had never spoken of it in absolute terms, James had hinted more than once that he understood her desire to make a match with Fezzi. Surely he wasn't unaware how fruitless her endeavors had proven to be thus far.

"May I ask," he said slowly, "have you two any kind of an understanding?"

The question brought immediate, pricking tears. Belle blinked furiously again. "No. That is, not exactly." Fezzi had never said the word "marriage" or "engagement." Nonetheless, she thought back to that night, and reheard his promise to her. "Yes." She drew in a deep breath. "Yes, he promised me!" The words rushed from her, growing in volume. "He said when he returned he would take me away, that I would never have to step inside Wilmington Bury again." Even blinking furiously she couldn't stop the tears blurring the sight of James watching her. Her voice was a whisper-yell now, but she couldn't seem to bank her need to tell him. "He never said marriage, but I believed that's what he meant. I've been waiting for years, placing all my hope on that Christmas when he said he'd take me away." Her fervor lessened; the words, now finally spoken aloud, took her zeal with them as they fled into the night. "But now…I don't know if he's forgotten, or if I misunderstood, or if he simply doesn't care anymore."

That was the most likely, that he'd ceased to care.

James stood in silence for a moment. Then, leaning in close, he asked in a soft voice, "Is there not someone else who might provide you with security and happiness?"

If only it were that simple. Belle shook her head decisively. "I have not had a Season, nor am I likely too. I love the country, but the society is not so very diverse, I'm afraid."

"But if you *were* to meet someone?"

Belle couldn't stop the course, barking laugh which escaped from her. "You mean, *should* I meet another man of wealth and title, and *should* he even notice me enough to wish to offer for me, and *should* this all happen before I'm well on the shelf?"

James shrugged his shoulders quite as if he expected *all* that to happen any day now. "It *is* possible."

Belle listed her head. "That you think so is flattering. But I have not your optimism." The cold bit against her nose and cheeks, but it didn't hurt nearly so much as the cold despair building inside her. "When a woman marries, her whole life becomes dependent on her husband's status and wealth. With it, he has the power to make her happy or unhappy, to make her life light or burdensome, pleasure or toil."

James pulled back, folding his arms and looking past her at the snow falling around them. "Is it important to you, then, that you marry a man with a title?" He said it quite nonchalantly, but there had been a subtle tightness to his tone that made Belle wonder.

"Yes," she answered honestly.

In a wave of understanding, Belle realized her misstep. James had no title; his grandfather's earldom had fallen to Fezzi, not him.

She reached a hand out, placing it against his arm. "Pray forgive me. I do not mean that gentlemen without titles are any less than those with them."

He didn't look back at her but his muscles tightened beneath her hand.

"Only, please understand," she hurried on—she would hate for him to misunderstand her on this point—"I am the daughter of a man with no title and no wealth. That has been the *only* definition others have labeled me by since my parent's death. It is all society cares for. Do you have any idea how I am treated when I'm introduced as 'Miss' instead of 'Lady'?"

He still wouldn't look at her. Belle dropped her hand and moved so that she stood directly in front of him. "My Aunt tolerates me, but that is all. My own cousin is forever throwing my lack of a titled father in my face." Her hands clenched as years of hurt, buried but not erased, built up inside her chest. "To finally be called 'Lady' is all I want. To walk into a room and have people *wish* to have me present, to *wish* to meet and speak with me." She drew in a deep breath, closing her eyes. "To not be a *nobody* anymore."

When she opened her eyes, James was watching her closely.

He cupped her face in one hand. "You are *not* a nobody."

His hand was warm, and she leaned into it slightly. She didn't feel like a nobody when she was with him. But that didn't change the fact that society was decidedly lacking in wonderful individuals like James. "I am, and, I am sorry to add, I will be forever unless I can marry someone titled."

James slowly shook his head, his thumb gently rubbing her cheek. "I, too, am sorry." He drew in a long breath. "You have no idea how sorry I am."

"That is kind of you, James. I understand if it doesn't make sense."

"I can't say that it does."

"That is because your cousin, Fezzi, respects you. So do the various other men you have dealings with, I assume. But you are a man, and as such, you are not as dependent upon what society thinks of you."

"Have I mentioned how much I dislike what society thinks?"

Belle smiled in spite of herself. "I can't say the topic has come up before."

"Then let me avail myself of this most apropos opportunity to state, most emphatically, that I firmly dislike what society thinks."

His sincerity mixed with a hint of levity did her heart a world of good. "You are a good man, James Radcliff." Belle went up on tiptoe and pressed a light kiss to his cheek. He smelled of pine boughs and musk, and Belle found she quite liked it.

"Dance with me?" he whispered, his mouth close to her ear.

Belle dropped back down off her toes. "But there's no music."

James inclined his head toward the door. "There is now."

Belle stopped to listen. Sure enough, soft strains of

Greensleeves drifted out from the manor. "I hadn't realized Miss Smith had begun playing."

James took a step back and then bowed low, extending one hand toward her. "Would you do me the honor, Lady Belle?"

His using the title 'Lady' was not lost on her. Belle curtsied as deep and elegantly as she could while still keeping the blanket he'd draped across her shoulders wrapped tightly around her. "I would be honored, Lord Radcliff, however"—she shot him a sassy smile—"I am already promised to another for this set."

He slowly came up, his brow twisted in a perplexed half-smile, half-scowl.

Belle giggled at the sight. "Yes, Lord Hammerstamp has already asked me." She indicated off to her right. Of course, no one *actually* stood there. James seemed more than a little confused. To help him, Belle jumped from the spot she was standing in, and landed on both feet in the snow, then jumped right back again. "Can you not see him standing just there?"

James glanced off at nothing and then back at her. "Hammerstamp?"

She pursed her lips. "You try and come up with a name on the spot, see if you do any better."

He jumped, just as she had, placing two solid footsteps in the snow a full stride away, and then jumped back. With a sweep of his arm, he motioned toward them. "May I introduce you to Miss Flabber-Steinwessel."

Belle looked at him with wide eyes.

He shrugged. "She's German."

"With footprints that big," Belle said, leaning toward him and whispering, "I would warn you not let her step on your feet."

James motioned toward Belle's "partner's" footprints. "With boots that size, your Mr. Hammerstamp must be as thin as a twig and a weakling at that."

"Yes," Belle enacted an elegant, ever-enduring sigh, "I am afraid that London is rather overrun with twigs this Season."

"You should have accepted my offer to dance instead of his," James said in an I-told-you-so tone.

"Hush, the dance is starting. And, as we are a Lord and Lady everyone is looking at us to make sure things are done properly."

Holding the blanket over her shoulders with one hand, Belle curtsied to her imaginary partner and then stretched out her one free hand, pretending to take hold of his, and spun in a circle, ending where she began.

James did much the same, even while speaking. "One would think, with as high titles as we both hold—"

"Oh, the highest, to be sure."

"—that we could do whatsoever we wished. Hang society and all that."

They continued on, moving about their pretend partners. "Ah, but would we not give rather the wrong impression to all the young, untitled individuals in the crowd? We are to set an example." She had to switch hands once or twice to execute the dance steps correctly. The third time, a corner of the blanket slipped off her shoulder completely.

She twisted, trying to catch it before it fell out of reach, but the corner evaded her. James stepped up and, taking both corners, tied them together. The end result was a rather large and unflattering knot against her collarbone, but it was effective.

"Thank you," she said, "but we best return to the dance. I fear we are holding up all the other dancers."

James let out a sudden grunt, half-falling forward suddenly. He caught Belle and twirled her around then seemed to regain his balance.

"I see what you mean," James said. "Your Mr. Hammerstamp nearly bowled me over. I have every notion to call him out."

"And ruin the evening?" They continued with the dance, Belle falling into line with James as they walked two steps forward, one step back, hand in hand.

"Ah, well if you put it that way, I shall simply endeavor to watch him all the more closely."

Belle tugged on his hand, bringing him in closer. "Perhaps you should start by letting go of my hand. It is well past time for the next step you know, and Mr. Hammerstamp is likely to call *you* out."

"Let him try," James said in a low, gruff voice.

"If not him, then surely Miss Flabber-Steinwessel will."

His brow dropped. "I see your point." He gave her hand a small squeeze and then released it. Soon, though, the dance brought them quite close together. Though the next step should have drawn them apart just as quickly, James lingered near her once more.

"If you continue in that fashion, Lord Radcliff," Belle said, unable to stop the smile he repeatedly brought to her face, "the papers are likely to be full of gossip regarding us tomorrow."

He moved about his own imaginary partner with grace; Belle couldn't ignore that she was looking forward to the next step which would bring them near one another again.

"I do believe," he said, turning in time with the music, "that I have already given you my opinion regarding what society thinks."

None too soon, the dance required that James and Belle meet in the center, palms and forearms together as they spun about in a small circle.

Belle adopted her most haughty tone. "You shock me, I'm sure."

Instead of stepping away, he wrapped his arm beneath the blanket hanging off her shoulders and around her waist, drawing her tight to him. "Suppose we gave society something to be truly 'shocked' about?"

Belle laughed. "We, sir, are bringing the dance to a complete halt around us."

"Precisely. Think of it as a charitable act."

"In what way is it charitable to ruin the dance for everyone?"

He hadn't let go and instead bent down, pressing his forehead against hers. "We're giving all the gossips in London something to do."

"Oh," Belle said. "Well, that is quite thoughtful of us."

"We are Lord and Lady, after all. Thoughtful is in our nature."

They swayed slowly to the music. Belle felt herself sigh as she leaned more heavily against him.

"Have I told you how grateful I am that you came to Easthill Manor for the winter holidays?" she asked.

"Are you grateful?"

"I don't think even I realized how much I needed a friend."

"Is that all we are?" His head shifted, and his nose brushed against hers. "Friends?"

Belle's breath caught. He was so near. The same pull she'd felt the night before returned, but with greater earnestness.

She couldn't be sure who initiated it, but the next moment his lips were against hers, and she returned the kiss. His arms held her close to him even as hers snaked up, and her fingers curled through his hair.

It was perfect. The snow fell gently, tiny bits of cold against her head and arms when all inside she felt so warm. His kiss reminded her of all the laughs they'd shared, all the comfort he'd given her.

A loud chord broke through the moment.

Good heavens, what was she doing? Belle pushed off

James, stumbling back two steps. She shook her head as if she could erase it all.

No. This wasn't right. This wasn't what she wanted.

Gracious, what if Fezzi had seen? She whirled around, but no one was around. He must still be seated with Miss Smith at the pianoforte. Thank goodness for that.

"Belle?"

She couldn't look at James. Her chest heaved. What had happened? What had possessed her?

What had possessed *him*?

"James, how could you?" He knew exactly what she hoped would come from this Christmas. She took another step closer to the door.

"Belle, please—"

She couldn't stay any longer. Lifting her skirt with one hand she ran toward the door. She slipped inside the music room, not bothering to glance over at Fezzi or Miss Smith. If they saw her, they said nothing. She continued through the room and out into the corridor.

Belle didn't slow until she was in her bedchamber, the door shut firmly behind her.

Why, oh why, had she allowed that to happen? She tugged at the ridiculous knotted blanket around her. Her hands trembled and her eyes filled with tears again, making it quite impossible to see what she was doing.

Finally the blanket dropped away. With her back against the closed door, Belle allowed herself to slip down to the floor where she sat, burying her head in her hands.

How could she have allowed such a thing to happen?

And what was she going to do about it now?

CHAPTER SEVENTEEN

James stood rooted to the spot well after Belle had fled from the balcony. Or, more truthfully, fled from *him*.

The cold night burned against his cheeks. Walking back toward the railing he placed both hands against it and leaned forward.

James, how could you?

Belle's hurt expression was burned into his memory. He surely would see it long after tonight. This was exactly why he had tried to avoid her company. This was why he hadn't wanted to attend the ball, why he hadn't wanted to dance with her before, and why he most certainly should not have followed her out onto the balcony.

With a growl, he folded his arms, resting his forearms against the railing and burying his head against them. What an idiot he was. What a muddleheaded dolt of a man. He shouldn't have let it happen.

Looking back, he couldn't be certain who'd initiated the kiss. It had been every bit as wonderful as he'd imagined it would be to kiss Belle. And, for a minute there, he'd felt certain she returned his ardor. What with the way she'd pressed up close to him and run her fingers through his hair. But, no, he must have been mistaken.

And all this, directly after she explicitly told him she wished only to marry a gentleman with a title. What had possessed him?

If not for Fezzi, he would have wrapped his arms around her days ago and not let go.

The cruel irony of the situation was not lost on James. If he had a title, it would solve all kinds of problems—one increasingly large complication in his life, at the very least.

Among the softly falling snow, a small voice inside him whispered that he *could* have a title.

Everything he'd heard about Mr. Thrup confirmed that what Mrs. Gaight had told him was true. Bringing such news to light would mean James would only be setting right what should have always been.

James stood up straight, smothering the thought. No, he would not continue to think in such a way. It would only lead to trouble. He rubbed his face a few times, willing good sense to enter his brain once more.

Of course, if the current Earl of Wilkins had acted with a bit more honor then none of them would have been in this place to begin with.

Likewise, if Fezzi had just returned from America as originally scheduled and married Belle, she would have been happy, and James never would have fallen for her. He would be blissfully ignorant, and she would simply be blissful.

James stalked toward the manor door, peering inside to the warm candlelight and elegant furnishings. Shaking his head, he stalked away, back across the balcony.

It galled him to think that Fezzi—who rarely laughed at Belle's jokes, who never bothered to seek her out, who hadn't once caught her tears or held her when she was feeling unequal to life—that *that* man was the one she wanted and the one who held the key to her happiness.

He moved toward the door once more. Was there not any justice in life? There Fezzi sat, still beside Miss Smith, with another woman fully depending upon him for her happiness. Was Fezzi busy with seeing to his promise to Belle? No. The man was, as Belle said, either ignoring her claim on him, had forgotten all about it, or simply had chosen not to care.

James ripped the door open and stomped inside. He headed straight for the pianoforte. Both Fezzi and Miss Smith looked up at him, their brows equally dropped in confusion.

True to form, before he could open his mouth, Miss Smith beat him to it. "Have you been speaking with Miss Young? She ran through here not twenty minutes ago. She seemed quite overwrought."

Yes. So he'd noticed. "Fezzi." His voice came out heavy. "I need to speak with you."

"If you wish it," Fezzi said. "We can speak in the den tomorrow."

"No. Now."

"Pardon me," Fezzi countered with an uncomfortable chuckle, "but we are rather in the middle of something. Can it not wait?"

James marched toward the door which led out to the corridor. "It cannot." He'd delayed this conversation far too long as it was.

Fezzi made his excuses to Miss Smith then stood and passed James as he moved out of the room. They walked in silence toward the den and waited a bit longer still until a few candles could be lit and the fire stoked.

"All right," Fezzi said, his tone turning far more impatient now that they were alone. "Let's have it."

James was sorely tempted to punch him in his impudent,

self-serving face. But that wouldn't help Belle, as much as it *would* make James feel better.

Standing directly in front of Fezzi, James began. "Did you promise Belle that you would marry her?"

Fezzi's eyes grew wide, and he rocked back slightly. "Ah, that." All the annoyance of a moment ago disappeared in a blink. Fezzi shook his head as he reached behind him for the large chair. He collapsed more than sat back into it. "I had rather wondered if she'd forgotten," he said slowly and barely loud enough for James to hear.

"Wondered?" James bit back, sitting across from his cousin. "Or hoped?"

Fezzi dropped his hands between his knees. "I don't know. Both?"

"Unless I am sorely mistaken, your mother raised you to be honorable."

The blow hit its mark; James saw it in Fezzi's brow and the hardness about his jaw.

"I was younger then," Fezzi said, shutting his eyes. "I was so excited for our trip across the ocean. I was two sheets to the wind that night, I fully admit it. Then I came upon Belle, crying and saying something about how she wished she could never return to Wilmington Bury." He placed both hands over his face. "The next morning I wasn't even sure I *had* said the things I thought I'd said. But then I saw Belle, and her eyes were filled with such light..."

James's fists tightened. He'd seen that light in Belle's eyes before; he knew exactly the expression Fezzi spoke of. To imagine her looking at *Fezzi* in the same way she'd begun to look at him—it was most maddening.

"Then why didn't you act as any true gentleman would and do as you promised?"

"I wanted to see America," he said, lamely. "I rationalized that, as soon as we returned, I would make good on my word.

But then one thing led to another, we stayed longer, and then longer still."

"We could have come back as originally planned," James broke in. "You never once so much as *hinted* that someone was awaiting your return."

"I know. I have no excuse for staying away so long."

"And Miss Smith? What excuse do you have for her?"

"Lud, James, it just happened. Surely you realize sometimes a man can't help but fall in love?"

Two notions struck James with equal, brutal force. So much so, he had to sit quietly for a moment to piece out exactly what he was feeling. First, this was the only time he'd ever heard Fezzi say 'love' in regard to anyone. The second was that James very much knew what it was like to fall in love when one didn't want to and was trying dashed hard not to.

"I told myself," Fezzi continued, "that Belle would surely be married by now. At the very least engaged. She was three years younger then too, and probably as happy as I that an ocean had kept us apart for so long."

"But that's not what happened." No matter James's feelings, Belle wanted Fezzi. He wouldn't let his own musings distract him from the purpose of this midnight meeting.

"Gads." Fezzi buried his head in his hands once more. "What am I going to do?"

James felt his full face alight with anger. "What are you going to do? I should think it would be obvious." He stood, towering over Fezzi. "You made an honorable woman a promise, one she has counted on for three years. It is time you did good by her." No matter how much it hurt James. No matter how certain he was that he could not stay at Easthill Manor to watch Fezzi court Belle. He needed to know she was happy. He needed to know she would have the life she deserved.

"Well?" James pressed.

Slowly, Fezzi nodded. "You are right, of course."

James spun on his heel and quickly left the room. He would stay only long enough to see Fezzi make good on his word. That, and he needed to find that blasted letter. But the moment those two things were settled, he would pack his bags and leave Easthill Manor for good.

CHAPTER EIGHTEEN

Belle considered hiding in her bedchamber all morning. But when she inquired after Lady Wilkins from her abigail, Belle learned that Fezzi's mother was already dressed and downstairs for breakfast. After so bad a headache as she'd had the night before, Belle was more than a little surprised and intently wished to see her to make sure for herself that the dowager was truly well.

She dressed quickly. Just before leaving her room, Belle's gaze landed on the few books which Mrs. Byrd had placed on her shelf, though they both knew they belonged in the library. Belle never had returned them, nor had she misplaced anything else in the manor for the housekeeper to find.

Such a thing seemed so petty just now. If Belle was to truly be a lady, she shouldn't be playing games with a servant. No lady would do such a thing. The realization saddened her, but there was no avoiding the truth. She would have to let this diversion go.

Leaving the books to themselves, Belle hurried down the stairs. Perhaps James would still be in his room. There was a very real chance he had as sincere a desire to avoid her as she did him.

Belle slipped up next to the breakfast room door but didn't move inside. Voices floated out and met her. Though she couldn't see anyone, Belle still knew each voice well enough to tell who was speaking.

"Are you certain you're feeling all right, Mother?" Fezzi asked.

"Yes," Lady Wilkins replied. "Quite well now, thank you."

But she didn't sound fully well. She sounded tired and drawn out. Her voice, normally strong and commanding, broke more than once during the sentence and was decidedly softer than usual. Belle chewed on her bottom lip. She'd never known Lady Wilkins to stay home from a long-anticipated evening, headache or no. And then, to rise the next morning sounding unwell...

Then again, Lady Wilkins *was* up. She was taking breakfast with the family, and at no late hour.

"I am sorry," Lady Wilkins continued, "to have ruined your evening. I hope you all were not terribly disappointed."

Belle's mind jumped to the kiss she had shared with James. A mottled mix of emotions warred within her at the memory. The kiss had been complete rapture, the moment all consuming. But as blissful as it had been, the realization which came crashing down afterward had been equally intense.

Muffled voices from the breakfast room brought Belle back to the present. She didn't know what she would do about James and the happenings of last night, but she very well couldn't stand out here all morning. Her stomach rumbled, seconding the motion that she move inside and eat.

"We are only glad that you are feeling better this morning."

Belle paused, hand up and ready to push the door open so that she may enter.

That had been James's voice. He *was* in the breakfast room.

Her lips twisted to the side. So much for hoping that he'd stayed hidden away for the morning.

The door swung open, and Belle found herself standing, framed by the doorway, in full view of the breakfast table. A manservant stood beside the open door; apparently he'd noticed her there and opened it for her. She gave him a small smile; it was William, one of the servants she'd spoken to from time to time.

Reluctant to join the table—though everyone was watching her—she took only a few steps in.

"How is your wife faring?" Belle asked William. With any luck, everyone else at the table would return to their conversation while she spoke with him. Then she could slip up to the table with as little attention as possible.

"Feeling better as of yesterday evening," William said with a bit of a relieved smile. "Doctor Lock says she's through the worst of it and should be right as rain soon enough."

"That is blessed news," Belle answered sincerely. William had been quite distressed only two days before over his wife's poor health. "Please convey to her my sincere pleasure at hearing of her return to health."

"Thank you, miss. I will." He gave her a bow and then returned to his post near the door.

Belle was left with nothing to do but face the room. The conversation around the table had started again; Fezzi was speaking to Lady Wilkins but Belle couldn't seem to force her brain to follow his words long enough to piece together what the topic was.

She moved up to the sideboard table without looking at anyone, most decidedly without looking at James. Belle glanced over the varied offerings of food. Hungry though she was, what were the chances she could stomach bacon and eggs? Not very good. Instead, she opted for only a bit of bread and preserves.

Belle sat at the empty chair beside Lady Wilkins. It was,

blessedly, nowhere near James. Less providential, she realized only after she sat, it was directly across from him.

"It is good to see you this morning, my dear," Lady Wilkins said to her.

"Thank you," Belle replied, turning toward the elderly woman and Fezzi, both on her right, to keep from looking at James. With none of the Smiths down so far this morning, it was only the four of them. "I must admit, I have been quite worried over you."

Lady Wilkins waved her concern away. "It was only a little headache."

Belle studied her closer. Only a little headache it may have been, but she looked worse for the wear. The wrinkles around her eyes seemed more prominent this morning, and her smile more forced. Belle's gaze dropped to the matron's plate; like her own, it held only a bit of toast and jam. Lady Wilkins had scarcely taken a bite.

Though Lady Wilkins said she was quite well, Belle wasn't at all sure she truly was.

"But tell me," Lady Wilkins said to them all, "how did you all entertain yourselves last night?"

Belle felt her face heat up. How could she respond to such a question?

Quite merrily, thank you. I especially enjoyed the part where James kissed me—or I kissed him. I'm still not sure which it was.

No, that would *not* go over well.

Belle reached for her cup of drinking chocolate to hide the fact that she had no answer to the simple question. James, too, seemed unwilling to respond.

After only a brief, albeit slightly awkward, moment of silence, Fezzi spoke. "We held our own ball, actually." He, too, sounded unsure what to say. Though why he should be hesitant Belle had no idea. "Geor—er, Miss Smith suggested it."

"Your own ball?" Lady Wilkins asked, her gaze moving quickly across each of them. "However did you manage?"

Clearly, Lady Wilkins had not missed the stiffness in the air, though how she would interpret it was anyone's guess.

Fezzi pushed his plate away and leaned forward. He chuckled, but it sounded fake. "The ladies took turns playing the pianoforte while the other one danced with either James or myself. It was all quite...lively."

"Indeed? Did not the ladies grow tired quickly? Playing one song and then dancing the next? It seems rather a lot to ask of any woman." Lady Wilkins's eyes landed on Belle and didn't leave.

Belle didn't dare pull the cup of drinking chocolate away from her mouth, instead taking one small sip after another. It may have appeared less than natural, but it certainly was better than setting the cup down and accidentally saying something she'd regret for the rest of her life.

Fezzi finally obliged and answered his mother yet again. "We only danced a couple of songs."

No one added to his simple statement.

Lady Wilkins sighed at length. "I see. Miss Smith is quite imaginative at times."

"Yes," Fezzi replied, his voice growing in warmth. "Quite the clever one. I must admit, she has repeatedly surprised me with her—"

James cleared his throat loudly.

The sudden sound from him brought Belle's gaze up. He was looking at Fezzi with something resembling a scowl. But why? His gaze shifted over and met hers.

His blue eyes were deep this morning, swirling with intense emotions she couldn't begin to sort out. His gaze dropped to her lips and hot awareness spread across Belle.

James looked down at his plate, breaking the brief connection.

What did he think of the kiss they'd shared last night? Her own angry words—*James, how could you?*—echoed about her head. Part of her was glad she'd said them. He had to have known she didn't want to be kissed by him.

Except, part of her *had* wanted it. That same part wished she could go back and erase those words even now. Perhaps, instead of speaking in anger, she could have stepped back into his arms. Even kissed him again.

"Belle." Fezzi spoke through the silence which had descended on the room. "It is my understanding that you haven't had the pleasure of a sleigh ride down Winsborough Lane this winter. I thought perhaps we might head out that way this afternoon."

Belle watched him closely; what exactly was he proposing?

Before she could answer, Fezzi continued. "Mrs. Smith is taking her three daughters into town for a bit of shopping and I remember that lane being a particular favorite of yours when covered in snow."

He was asking for a ride, with her, alone?

Good heavens. It was exactly the sort of thing she'd been hoping for all month long. An outing, just them. Precisely what she'd dreamed about.

And, gracious, her mouth was hanging open. Belle shut it, replacing her idiotic gape with a smile. "I would be delighted." He did mean just the two of them, right? She wouldn't show herself to be a ninny and ask outright, but if she was understanding him correctly that was what he meant. It would be—

The sound of James's cup scraping against the table brought everyone's eye to him. He scooped up the cup, drained it of its contents, and slammed it back onto the table. With a hard shove, he pushed away from the table, stood, and stomped out of the room without a glance or farewell to anyone.

Belle twisted in her chair, watching him pass through the

doorway and out of sight down the corridor. He was upset, that much was clear. She hated knowing that he was partially upset *with her*. Belle felt the prick of tears against the back of her eyes.

She blinked them away. He had no right to be upset with her. She hadn't asked for his affections, nor had she sought them. He was fully aware she hoped for an understanding with Fezzi. She wasn't going to wallow or quake because he was moping.

Belle turned back to Fezzi. "I have been hoping to see Winsborough Lane."

"Excellent." Fezzi seemed as willing to ignore James's brooding departure as she was. "Shall we plan on four o'clock?"

"That sounds delightful."

Fezzi gave her a small smile, though it appeared a bit forced, then stood and left as well.

Only Lady Wilkins and Belle remained at the table. The weight of the conversation didn't dissipate. Belle was quite thrilled that Fezzi had finally asked to spend time with her. Rather, she at least felt she *would* have been thrilled if she could only get James's sour expression out of her head.

"It seems," Lady Wilkins said under her breath, "that more than dancing happened last night."

Belle's only response was to take a long sip of her chocolate. Gracious, if Lady Wilkins only knew.

CHAPTER NINETEEN

Winsborough Lane a week ago, a breathtaking ride on horseback a few days later, sitting close to one another during church services the day after that, trips into Dunwell, strolls about the snow-covered hedges, and today Fezzi and Belle were spending the afternoon preparing the Christmas boxes to be handed out to tenants and servants in a few days' time. More than that, for the entire week, after dinner he'd sat beside her and spoken almost exclusively to her. During the day, when they crossed each other in the corridors, he took interest in what she was about.

Belle could hardly believe her good luck. It seemed Fezzi had finally remembered his promise—finally remembered *her*.

Though the Smiths were all still about, they had taken to visiting shops and neighbors quite a lot as of late. In the evenings, they all retired early. Miss Smith especially seemed to be forever finding excuses to not be about.

Belle tried to sit still as her abigail twisted a bit of red ribbon into her hair. It was, perhaps, a bit much for an afternoon preparing boxes, but Belle was feeling festive. Besides, now that Fezzi was taking the time to notice her, she didn't intend to waste even a simple afternoon inside.

Through the mirror, Belle could see the trunk sitting at the foot of her bed. She hadn't opened it for nearly a week. Fezzi had mentioned yesterday, yet again, that he saw her little puppet show as *quaint*, though it had been clear to her what he actually meant was *pointless*. Was it any wonder he had refused to truly see her for so many years when she was repeatedly engaging in such foolishness? How could he have ever seen her as a lady when she'd been acting as a child all along?

Ladies of the *ton* did not put on puppet shows.

Her gaze remained frozen on the trunk. Her heart ached to go to it, pull the lid open, and hold her small creations. She had been quite excited at how her forest beast had turned out.

But, no. She was endeavoring to show to Fezzi that she could be a countess, a proper wife to an earl. If that meant giving up an insignificant puppet show, then so be it. She would let Lady Wilkins know of her change in plans before meeting up with Fezzi.

Once her abigail was finished, Belle thanked the young woman and then made her way to Fezzi's den. Now, if only she could get James out of her head. What a nincompoop she was proving to be. Finally Fezzi was interested in her, or at least acting as though he was, and she could barely go ten minutes at a time without her mind wandering to James. The times they'd laughed, the times he'd held her, and of course, the time they'd kissed.

Turning the corner, Belle pulled up short.

As though her thoughts had conjured him, James stood before her. He wasn't smiling; she hadn't seen his smile since they'd danced on the balcony.

Belle glanced up at his face but couldn't seem to hold his gaze. Her eyes traveled back down to their feet, only centimeters between them.

She didn't speak, and neither did he, the pregnant silence between graceless and awkward. Still, she didn't want to leave. Even with waves of tension rolling off him, Belle was drawn toward James.

Good heavens, but she'd missed him. Tears blurred her vision. For days now they'd been ignoring one another, forever standing on opposite sides of the room, leaving a conversation if the other was drawn into it.

"James," she whispered. Who would have guessed it would take so much effort to say one simple word?

Without a sound, he stepped to the side, moving around her, and disappeared down the corridor.

Finding herself suddenly alone, Belle drew in a deep breath. He'd taken most of the strain with him when he'd left, but traces of it still threaded around her chest, making her heart hurt. Shaking her head, wishing she could somehow fix whatever was broken between them, Belle hurried down the stairs.

Lady Wilkins was in the morning room, a bit of stitching atop her lap. Seeing the needle and thread, Belle almost held her tongue. Her poor little puppets; they would never be finished, after all. She closed her eyes and squared her jaw. She wanted Fezzi to come up to scratch, didn't she? Of course she did. If she wanted him, then she may have to give up a few of her more inane diversions; that was certainly not too much to ask.

Belle walked up to Lady Wilkins who greeted her kindly. In a few words, Belle explained that she had decided not to put on the performance this year. Lady Wilkins seemed surprised but didn't press the point. Before anyone could convince her otherwise—most particularly, her own heart—Belle hurried out of the room and toward Fezzi's den.

She entered the room and found the desk and half the

space filled with opened boxes. Fezzi stood in the middle of it, scratching the back of his neck.

She'd not set foot in this room for the past few years; with no Lord Wilkins in residence she'd not had reason to. Stepping into the room now, Belle couldn't help but reminisce. Like every other room in the manor, Belle had so many memories associated with this den. "I can vividly remember your father sitting at that desk."

Fezzi looked up at her, a moment of surprise widening his eyes. He glanced over at the desk and then back to her. "I confess, I remember the same most days. I see him, sitting there, answering letters or meeting with his man of business."

Belle leaned against the door frame, her gaze leaving the desk and traveling over the many, many empty boxes filling the room now. "It appears we have quite the afternoon ahead of us."

Fezzi blew out a long, slow breath. "To own the truth, I'm only now realizing that the den may not prove to be the best space in which to organize so many boxes."

Belle pulled her lips to the side. "Perhaps if we only do a few boxes at a time? Then we can have the servants remove those and we can do the next batch."

Fezzi nodded. "Which boxes should we start with?"

He never had been the best at organizing. "We should probably start with boxes that are all the same and most easy to assemble."

He looked at her, his expression skewed by uncertainty, and slowly shrugged.

A small part of her brain commented that Miss Smith *did* rather go well with Fezzi in one respect; she was quite good at coordinating those things that he desperately needed help placing in order.

Belle quieted that thought immediately. "How many boxes will be going to men without families? Those will undoubtedly not need to be so big, and so they'll be easier to assemble while the room is still so...full." There probably wouldn't be as many either.

"Good thinking." Fezzi looked and sounded relieved.

If Fezzi ever did come up to scratch, Belle would probably have years of this before her—organizing and coordinating most activities, helping remind him of previously laid plans and of tenants or servants who needed his attention.

No, Belle assured herself, not *if* they made a match. *When.* Most decidedly *when.*

For the next couple of hours, they placed items in boxes, then moved the filled boxes to the corridor where a couple of footmen collected them, while Fezzi and Belle repeated the process. It was comfortable. Fezzi and she had always had an easy friendship. Though, she couldn't help but notice that the pull she'd felt around James *was* lacking.

As the sun began to set, Fezzi sat back on his heels. "Drat; I think that's the end of the twine."

Belle glanced over at the small bit left in his hands. That pitiful length would never be enough to tie shut the remaining boxes. "If I'd known you weren't going to bring enough, I would never have worn a ribbon in my hair for fear you might use it instead."

Fezzi's brow creased and he tilted his head. Clearly, her tease had not been nearly as witty as she'd imagined it.

James would have laughed. But James was not present. He was in some other room in Easthill Manor avoiding her. And she was here in the den, avoiding him.

Fezzi pushed to a stand. "I'll go ask Mrs. Byrd for some more." With nothing more than that, he left.

Belle stood as well and walked over to the remaining few boxes. They'd made good progress today. At the beginning, she'd wondered if they'd ever see the floor again. But slowly and surely, they'd made their way down the rows of boxes, filling them a few at a time. Placing the last remaining items in the boxes, Belle stepped back.

There was nothing left to do until Fezzi returned with the twine. Placing her hands behind her back, Belle twisted gently from side to side, causing her skirt to twirl about her legs. If James were here, they'd—

No. She stopped the thought before it formed.

James *wasn't* here, and she *didn't* wish him here. She was quite content spending time with Fezzi. This was everything she'd hoped for.

Nonetheless, as she thought the words, they felt hollow.

Stilling herself, Belle looked about the room. Surely there was something in here for her to do until Fezzi returned? Her eyes landed on the grand desk, the one the late Lord Wilkins had sat behind every day she'd visited Easthill Manor as a girl.

Fezzi's words returned. *I see him, sitting there, answering letters.*

James was still looking for a letter, wasn't he? Surely he'd tell her if he'd found what he sought; she knew he wasn't a man to give up. Stepping toward the doorway, she peered out into the corridor. It was empty. She couldn't hear any steps coming from either direction. She leaned back into the room, her eyes traveling toward the desk.

She had several minutes alone, at least. James and she had searched the upstairs but never in here. Belle reached out and pulled a drawer open. Gracious, but searching a man's desk felt far more like invading personal space than searching through old tables ever had. James would have told her if he'd already looked here, wouldn't he?

Belle stood, nearly frozen, peering inside the drawer. James had insisted what he was doing was of paramount importance. If he insisted it was, then she believed him.

Steeling herself, Belle reached inside the drawer and began pushing papers around. No letters were inside. She moved on to the next drawer down. The further she searched, the more expeditiously she moved. Finishing the drawers on one side, she moved to the other.

In the last drawer, Belle found a large ledger. When she pulled it out, a single letter lay in the bottom of the drawer, worn and yellow with time. The front lettering showed it to be addressed to Fezzi's father. After setting the ledger on the chair beside her, Belle picked up the letter. The seal had been broken some time ago, but pieces of the wax still clung to the paper.

Belle gently unfolded the letter. Her gaze dropped to the bottom signature; it was written by Lady Wilkins. Feeling quite like an intruder, but unable to stop herself all the same, Belle quickly read the top few lines.

I hardly know where to begin.

You will hate me, I know. I only beg you read this in its entirety. I make no excuses; what I have done is wrong. It is a sin against you and against God.

Belle read, hardly able to breathe. Nothing was stated overtly, but there was no mistaking what Lady Wilkins was writing. Fezzi was not the late Lord Wilkins's son. Lady Wilkins expressed her sincere distress, stating only that she had grown intolerably lonely in Lord Wilkins's continued absence. But she also expressed a willingness to be held fully accountable for her actions going so far as to say: *If you must hate me, then I will accept it as my penitence in this life. Only, I beg you not to hate the child, nor turn him out. It is not his fault. If you must send someone away, send me.*

"There's no twine in there."

Fezzi's voice broke through the still room like glass crashing against stone. Belle snapped her mouth shut and hid the letter behind her back. Schooling her features, she stood and faced him.

"No," she said, her voice shaking, "I haven't found any."

"Never mind though," Fezzi said, his own gaze on the few remaining boxes. "Mrs. Byrd is sending some up."

She could only stare at him. Did he know? Had either of

his parents ever told him the truth? Good gracious, the man she'd always thought of as his father wasn't truly his father at all.

He looked at her, and his brow dropped. "Are you feeling all right, Belle?"

"I am perhaps tired."

He nodded, his gaze once more moving to the remaining boxes. "We have worked hard this afternoon."

She couldn't stay. If she remained in the same room as him, she would slip and say something, she was certain. "Fezzi," she said, "would you mind finishing up without me?"

"No problem at all. You go lie down and rest before dinner."

"Thank you." She slipped out from behind the desk and moved straight for the doorway. "I think I shall."

But resting was the last thing on her mind as Belle moved out into the corridor, the letter clasped tightly in her hand.

CHAPTER TWENTY

*J*ames slumped yet further down against the pleasant settee facing the equally pleasant fire. But today, he was unable to enjoy either. The bedchamber he had been granted the use of while staying at Easthill Manor was by no means spartan. Indeed, the bedclothes were thick and warm, the curtains rich in color, and the furniture quite comfortable. Nonetheless, he hadn't been spending nearly every moment of every day for the past week in here because he enjoyed the surroundings. There was no denying it. He was hiding.

James tipped his head back until it rested against the back of the settee and draped an arm over his eyes. He'd been tempted, when coming upon Belle unexpectedly in the corridor earlier that day, to take her in his arms and kiss her soundly. But no. He exhaled deeply. Her reaction the previous week was more than enough motivation to never try such a thing again.

Still, he thought about it. He couldn't seem to shake the memory of her lips against his. And the way she felt pressed up against him. It was as though she was made to be there; they fit so perfectly together. He could have sworn that she'd leaned into the kiss every bit as much as he had—at least at first.

With a groan, he turned and laid fully down across the cushions. Lady Wilkins would have been upset to see his boots atop her beautiful furniture, no doubt. But right now, he couldn't seem to care. Not that she'd ever know anyway. He planned on remaining in this room until it was absolutely necessary to venture out again. Then he'd only leave for the shortest amount of time.

Blast—watching Fezzi offer over breakfast that first morning after their kiss to take Belle for a ride had been maddening. It had only gotten worse after that. He'd lost track of all the outings and activities the two had done since. Mostly, he'd taken to ignoring everything but his own comings and goings. Granted, James had all but demanded Fezzi do it. But that didn't mean he had to like it.

James tilted his head, his gaze moving to the low-burning fire. He was a little surprised a servant hadn't already come to stoke it. If one didn't come to stoke it soon, he'd have to summon someone. Either that or sit in the dark.

Not that it would matter either way.

A soft rap came from the door.

It seemed the servants at Easthill Manor were not entirely incompetent. Only a bit delayed was all.

"Enter," he called, not bothering to stand.

The door creaked slightly as it swung open.

"James?"

James sat up directly, his boots slamming against the floor. "Belle?" Gads, what was she doing *here*? In his *bedchamber* of all places?

She shut the door silently behind her. James stood. What was she about? This was beyond the pale.

"Belle, you have to leave."

She didn't respond, didn't even look at him, but slowly

walked toward him. A heated awareness coursed over him. The urge to hold her came too, as strong waves crashing again his form. Despite the overwhelming urges, he was still cognizant of the danger she'd put herself in.

"If we're found, you would be ruined," he pressed. She had to leave. He'd hurt her the other night; he wouldn't do it again.

She moved directly up to him, still not meeting his gaze.

James took a large step backward. Drawing himself up, he spoke in as firm a voice as he could manage, reeling though he was. "You have to go. Now."

Slowly, her head came up.

There were tears in her eyes. Her skin looked strangely ashen. James's heart lurched forward. What had happened? Was she all right?

Finally she spoke, but her voice was fragile. "I think I found what you've been looking for."

His gaze dropped to her hand. She held out a folded sheet of paper. A letter.

At the sight, new emotions washed over him. These ones were cold and trailed along his skin like fingers of ice. He ran a hand down his face. He'd almost begun to think he would never find the letter—never find the dreaded proof he'd sought.

She still held it out to him, but he couldn't seem to force himself to take it. Shaking his head, he swore softly. He'd hoped, he'd prayed for weeks now to find nothing. To be able to return home after the winter season with a clear conscious that no one could ever hurt Fezzi.

"Did you read it?" he asked.

Belle nodded.

James felt as though he might be sick. Nonetheless, he finally reached out and took the letter. With a flick, he opened it. If the color of the paper was any indicator, it was old. He read through the contents quickly, his stomach rolling all the more violently as he did so.

The letter was every bit as condemning as he'd been afraid it would be.

"What does this mean for Fezzi?" Belle asked, her voice still small and frail.

James shook his head and collapsed back onto the settee. "The stipulations regarding the Wilkins earldom are quite clear." He lifted the letter a bit higher. "This would ruin him."

"Oh my," Belle sighed as much as spoke. She slowly lowered herself, sitting beside him.

"Where did you find it?"

"In the old desk in the den."

Of course. "Where the late Lord Wilkins conducted all his business."

"Yes."

He should have known to search there first. Only, Mrs. Gaight said *she* had been in possession of the letter. The dear woman had grown rather forgetful in her old age. Perhaps she'd only been told of the letter but never possessed it herself? Perhaps she'd returned it later? Or slipped it back into the desk without telling a soul? He would never know. Not that it mattered. "I take it you've shown this to no one but me."

She faced him directly, a single eyebrow arching up. "I came straight here the moment I found it. You don't honestly believe I would..."

"No, of course not." James pressed his lips into a thin line. Belle would never do anything to hurt another. More than that, though... "I'm certain you would never do anything to strip Fezzi of his title. That's why you want him, after all." The moment the words left his mouth he knew it'd been wrong to say them. They were hurtful, sour words. Still, he almost didn't regret it.

Belle's face hardened, her cheeks flaming pink and her brow compressed into an angry line.

"How dare you," she hissed.

A small part of him could not deny that she was beautiful when furious. He gave the thought a vindictive shove and looked toward the fire instead. "Did you not say as much yourself out on the balcony?"

She shot to her feet, fists hanging at her sides. "I don't want to see Fezzi hurt. Don't you dare twist my words to mean anything else."

"Tell me, this title and wealth you seek, can it cheer and comfort you in times to come?" *He* most certainly would have if given half a chance.

Belle's mouth screwed up into a tight pucker. "Spiteful man." Spinning on her heel, she practically flew to the door but paused once she got there. "James Radcliff, promise me *you* don't intend to ruin Fezzi."

Did she truly think he would?

James ran both hands through his hair. Perhaps it was the result of being too long in his room alone with nothing but his thoughts for company, perhaps it was the knowledge that he was losing her and that she didn't feel as he did. Either way, James stood, his anger directing his words more than his mind. "You fear the world too much, Belle. I have seen your nobler aspirations fall off one by one, as this singular, master-passion engrosses you."

Her nose scrunched up and her lips pressed together tightly. "I don't know what you're talking about."

"When was the last time you worked on your puppets? Or hid another knickknack for Mrs. Byrd? You are losing *you*, Belle." His anger was burning out, leaving only a hollowed-out longing in its place. "Please, I can't stand to watch you do this any longer."

"Oh, James..." she sputtered for a minute and, much to his dismay, her eyes filled with tears.

Lud, he shouldn't have said those things. He was frustrated and wound tight with all that had happened. Still, she didn't deserve his harsh comments. He took a step toward her, but before he could go further, Belle flung the door open and ran from the room.

James stopped. His door slammed shut and the bang echoed about the empty space.

He ought to go apologize. He'd let his anger get the better of him—anger at learning the truth regarding Lady Wilkins, anger at knowing it was his responsibility now to protect a man who spent most of his days delighting in nonsensical diversions. Most of all, his anger at being reminded, yet again, that Belle wanted Fezzi, not him.

He could apologize, but that wouldn't change who Belle wished to be with. He briefly visualized a sincere plea for her forgiveness. Somehow he couldn't see himself doing it and *not* reaching for her at the same time. As he closed his eyes, James's shoulders slumped.

Perhaps this was for the better. With her furious at him, James would have an even easier time avoiding another misstep such as that deuced kiss. He missed her though. She'd not left his presence two minutes ago, and he already missed her. What he wouldn't do to give her one last kiss. Slowly he made his way to his armoire and flung the door open, intent on secreting the letter away. He would figure out the best, safest next step later. Now that he had the letter in his possession, there was no need to rush. He would need a clear head to decide on what should happen now. Kneeling, James pulled out his trunk and flung it open.

There, resting safely in the bottom, was the elegant box he'd purchased for Belle. He didn't have to open it to know four spools of thread were tucked inside. He ground his jaw and shoved the letter down next to it. Then he slammed the trunk closed.

Cursing titles and wishing all thread to the devil, James stood and headed back to the settee. He paused before sitting and stared down at it instead. He was beginning to hate this piece of furniture.

Consigning himself to a miserable end of the Christmas holidays, he dropped onto it once more.

Might as well get comfortable; he had a feeling he would be hiding in here quite a bit over the next couple of weeks.

CHAPTER TWENTY-ONE

*H*ow dare he.

Thinking that Belle only wished to protect Fezzi for her own benefit. Hinting that she cared more for the Wilkins title than for Fezzi himself. Belle fumed the entire rest of the day. All night long, she tossed and turned, reliving the conversation and the fury she had felt at James's words. He claimed she was losing herself—what did he even mean by such a thing? If anything, she was finally securing her own future, embracing all she'd hoped for.

Morning came with a cloudy sky which matched her mood. Even two hours spent alone with Fezzi playing chess did nothing to brighten her spirits.

Eventually, Fezzi excused himself, saying he'd twisted James's arm and finally convinced his cousin to go out riding. He asked if she cared to join them, but upon hearing that James was counted as one of the party, she refused and instead insisted she'd rather join his mother during her at-home today.

So it was, only an hour after both gentlemen had left the house, Belle found herself sitting across from two other ladies of the neighborhood.

She'd not said much for the entire quarter of an hour, and their visitors didn't seem to mind. They dropped a few hints which clearly showed that she wasn't exactly needed nor wanted in the conversation.

Belle hadn't had a London Season, so certainly she couldn't be trusted to understand just how unfashionable violet ribbon was just now. Belle had never made her bows, so she certainly couldn't comprehend the stress and strain of being forever among the *haut ton*. Belle's father never held a seat in Westminster, so she couldn't possibly fathom the complex issues their country was facing.

Lady Wilkins did her best to counter the subtle attacks. Belle loved her all the more for it. Still, some things could not be changed.

She was almost relieved when Miss Smith walked into the room and sat beside her. Her arrival in England may have upended Belle's hopes for her future, but Miss Smith had never been cruel to Belle. Truth was, Belle had come to rather enjoy Miss Smith's company, exhausting though it was at times. She was a kind, considerate woman, one who Belle would be pleased to call friend. Only, with all that stood between them, Belle didn't know if such could ever be.

While one of their neighbors continued to speak on and on regarding how unjust it was that silk was so hard to come by, Miss Smith leaned in toward Belle.

"Would you take a turn about the room with me?" she asked.

Belle was not at all sure she wanted to hear what Miss Smith wished to say. Miss Smith had been strangely absent from the house nearly every day as of late. The excuses were always that she had plans with her family to see or do something outside of Easthill Manor. What could Miss Smith have to say to her now?

Nonetheless, Belle wouldn't be unkind to the woman who

had never been such to her. "That would be delightful," she whispered back.

Neither of the neighbors seemed to notice when Belle and Miss Smith stood and moved to walk about the room. It was quite a relief to be free of the conversation and for several steps, Miss Smith seemed unwilling to start a new one.

Finally though, as they neared the far side of the room, Miss Smith glanced over at the visiting ladies and then turned back to Belle.

"I need to tell you something," she said only loud enough for Belle to hear.

"Very well." Judging by her tone, this was not to be a light-hearted tête-à-tête.

"The other night, after our impromptu ball, James demanded to speak with Fezzi."

He had? That had to have happened just after the kiss. Even now, the memory heated her cheeks.

"They left, but Fezzi returned soon. He spoke to me..." She hesitated for a moment, but then her words rushed out. "He told me of his promise to you. He told me that, as a gentleman, he was beholden to follow through. I agree—I think it very important that a man do as he promised." She stopped suddenly, her gaze jumping toward the visiting ladies, then she continued softer once more. "What I'm trying to say is"—she pulled herself up—"I'll not stand in your way."

Before Belle could respond, Miss Smith hurried from the room.

THE NEIGHBORS LEFT AFTER A FULL THREE-QUARTERS OF AN hour, and Lady Wilkins retired to her room for a bit of rest before dinner. Still, Belle remained in the drawing room, mulling over what Miss Smith had said.

It seemed she had not been mistaken that Fezzi was finally willing to fulfill his promise to her. Even more surprising, she now knew she had James to thank for it.

Dear, sweet, maddening James.

Belle felt certain she ought to be elated; her hopes were finally being realized, after all. And she'd been hoping for this for ever so long. But sitting in the large brocade wingback by a slowly dying fire, all she could feel was sad.

And a bit confused.

And quite tired.

She yawned. It was no wonder after all the tossing and turning the previous night. It wasn't as though she'd awoken well rested. She snuggled against the wing of the chair, her head pressed against the padded fabric. It would probably be wisest to retire to her room for a rest as Lady Wilkins had. If she were to become a true lady soon, she probably ought to learn their methods. Who better to learn from than Fezzi's mother?

Slowly her eyes closed as the heat from the fire lapped over her hands and legs. The gentlemen would be returning from their ride soon. She could clearly imagine James, sitting tall on a midnight-black horse. Of course, she didn't know what kind of mount he rode. He'd been on foot when they'd met him in town that one day. Heavens, but that felt like ages ago.

Prancing visions of James on horseback. Tumbling echoes of the passion she'd felt that night on the balcony. His smile. The feel of his arms around her. They all mingled together, leaving bursting bits of light dancing across her eyelids.

They were chased by heavy memories of the past few days. Her arraignment, his accusations. A shiver skittered down her spine. Belle pulled her feet up onto the seat cushion, tucking them beneath her. Why was she suddenly so cold? Where was the warmth of those previous memories?

She tried to pull them back to her—the times she and

James had laughed, the times he'd comforted her. Notwithstanding, shadows of more recent memories lurked in the corners, never fully gone.

A weight laid gently down on her shoulders, bringing much-needed warmth. Her fingers twitched, brushing up against thick fabric. A blanket. She sighed and tugged it closer around her shoulders and under her chin. Already she was feeling more comfortable. Perhaps now the shadows would leave her dreams.

Even less than half awake, Belle became aware of a presence. Someone leaned over her. Drew nearer. Pressed a soft kiss to her forehead.

Sleep fled like birds taking flight. Stunned, Belle felt unable to move, unable to open her eyes even. What was a lady supposed to do when she found herself in a situation such as this? Had it been Fezzi? Somehow she couldn't fathom him doing such a thing.

James, then? But he'd been clearly avoiding her for days. And who could blame him after the things they'd said to one another? Still, she couldn't help but wish it was him.

Summoning all her courage, Belle pried first one eye and then the other open. A deep red blanket was draped over her and the fire had, indeed, burned low.

But apparently she'd opened her eyes too late. Other than herself, the drawing room was completely empty.

CHAPTER TWENTY-TWO

Dinner that night was an uncomfortably quiet affair.
Lady Wilkins had chosen not to come back down after all and was dining in her room. As was James, apparently, since he too was absent from the table. The entire Smith family was present, but they hardly said a half-dozen sentences between them.

Fezzi tried to be a good host; Belle could respect his valiant attempts. He smiled and agreed with anything anyone said. He even tried to add a comment or two of his own here and there. But none of the topics brought up lingered for more than a sentence or so before fading away into silence.

Miss Smith was exceptionally quiet. Belle watched her closely. She, who usually spoke much, seemed disinclined to conversation tonight.

Truth was, it made Belle sad to see the warmhearted woman so distraught. It made her feel rather like an ogre.

But, didn't Belle deserve some happiness in life too? Didn't Fezzi's promise to her mean something? Was it very wicked of her to be happy he was finally making good on his word?

Perhaps it was. After all, who was she that the heavens would smile on her wishes? She was not titled nor wealthy. Miss Smith may not have come from a titled father either, but she was American and that changed things. Miss Smith was clearly wealthy, besides, and most certainly a woman of high standing.

She wasn't a nobody like Belle was.

Belle stabbed a beet and shoved it into her mouth. She *wouldn't* be a nobody after she married Fezzi. Instead of Miss Young, she would be Lady Wilkins—a true lady of consequence in the eyes of the *ton*. No doubt Fezzi would take her to London for the Season if she asked. He was certainly a kind man. She could not do better than him.

Except, behind his smile, he looked so sad.

Miss Smith did too.

And what of James? She hadn't seen him all day. Was he dining alone, his eyes swirling with loneliness or even possibly regret?

Belle suddenly had no appetite. She set her fork down gently so as not to make a sound and draw attention to herself. Why was it that now, when her hopes were finally within reach, she felt so bleak?

The dining room door opened suddenly. A footman bowed. "Lady Wilmington and Lady Harriet to see Miss Young, my lord."

Aunt Agnes and Harriet were here? Belle glanced over at Fezzi; his face showed as much surprise as she felt. She had no time to recover, however, for in that very moment, the two women Belle wished least to see swept into the room.

Belle had never seen Aunt Agnes's nose quite so high in the air. "Come, Belle," she ordered. "We've come to take you home."

"Home?" Belle echoed.

"Yes." Her aunt turned toward the footman who'd just showed them in. "Instruct Miss Young's abigail to have her things packed and ready for removal back to Wilmington Bury within the hour."

The footman bowed once more and then left the room. Belle's head swam. What were her aunt and cousin doing? They weren't supposed to return from the Duke of Pembroke's Christmas house party for almost two weeks yet.

"Don't just sit there," Aunt Agnes snapped. "I'm most serious about leaving within the hour. Your cousin and I have had a very trying time of it, and we wish to be in our own beds before midnight."

Belle slowly stood. But what had happened with His Grace? Her gaze moved from her aunt to her cousin. Harriet's face was more flushed than usual, and her lips were pulled into a tense line.

Belle moved up closer to her aunt and kept her voice low. "I could always remain for another night and then return to Wilmington Bury in the morning. If you are exhausted, there's no reason to wait on me."

"Nonsense," Aunt Agnes clipped. "Lady Wilkins has been kind to watch after you while we were at Pembroke. Now that we have returned, early though it may be, we cannot trespass on her goodwill any longer."

Belle colored at the statement. *To watch over her?* It sounded as though Belle were nothing but a child, ill-suited to being left home alone.

Aunt Agnes turned and hurried after a passing maid, calling to the young girl to help Belle's abigail rush things along. Belle was left standing, in full view of everyone at the table, next to Harriet. Oh, why did her family have to come now? Come and ruin everything?

Harriet was silent, but her eyes were full of vexation and a thin line of tears hovered along her bottom lashes. She appeared genuinely upset.

"Did you enjoy your trip?" was all Belle could think to ask.

Harriet's expression turned ugly. She leaned in slightly and hissed, "Hang Christmas. And if I can't have a man who comes up to scratch, then neither shall you." With that, she stalked back toward her mother.

Belle could not remember ever seeing either of them so enraged. Something truly distressing must have taken place at Pembroke—nothing less would have convinced Harriet to give up on her ardent attempts to ensnare the Silent Duke. The next forty minutes passed in a blur. Manservants and maids rushed about. Belle's trunks were brought down post haste. She had not thought it possible, but in less than an hour from the time her relatives stormed into Easthill Manor, Belle was standing at the door, pelisse and bonnet on and bags packed. She could only hope that nothing had been left behind.

Fezzi stood beside her. "I had not thought our little party would be dispersing so soon," he said.

"Nor I." She tried to affect a cheerful, unconcerned demeanor, though she doubted anyone was fooled.

"Shall I call on you in two days' time?"

Even now, with all that was happening around her, Belle was not ignorant of the fact that Fezzi had just uttered words she'd dreamed of hearing from him for years. Nor was she ignorant of the truth. His words did nothing to her heart.

"I should very much enjoy it if you did," she responded. She tipped her head slightly in Harriet's direction. "I believe I shall be in grave need of a distraction."

"Distraction? Or escape?"

"Whatever you are able to provide, I will accept."

At her words, something shifted inside Fezzi's gaze. She felt it in her stomach, too. Just like that, they weren't talking about his visit in two days' time. They were talking about something far more long term.

Fezzi didn't smile.

Belle found she couldn't either.

He took a small step away, then turned and faced her fully. "Well, I am glad for the time you were able to stay with us this year. Travel home safely."

She thanked him and curtsied most politely.

Aunt Agnes came up from behind Belle and curtsied her farewell. Immediately after, she took hold of Belle's hand, physically pulling her down the stairs and away from Easthill Manor.

"Curse the duke and his house party," she muttered now that they were out of hearing. "I swear he issued invitations just so he could parade that little insignificant chit before us all."

Feeling it best to remain silent on the matter, Belle dutifully followed her aunt and cousin into the night. As her relatives situated themselves in the carriage, Belle turned back around. Her gaze moved up the steps and back toward Easthill Manor.

Fezzi remained not far inside, the Smiths a few paces behind him. But even further past them, halfway up the stairs, stood James. He watched her, his blue eyes swirling. He looked confused, as well he might since he hadn't been in the dining room when her aunt had unexpectedly shown up and demanded Belle return to Wilmington Bury. Still, there was something else in his gaze too, something Belle couldn't quite discern.

His intense gaze was the last thing she saw as the door to Easthill Manor closed with a click.

TWO DAYS LATER, FEZZI VISITED AS HE'D SAID HE WOULD. After a short turn about the snow-blanketed garden at Wilmington Bury, Fezzi brought up his promise of years ago. He acknowledged he had meant marriage, though he'd never spoken that word specifically. He apologized for not behaving more honorably and for the awkward situation he'd thrust her into this Christmas by inviting the Smith family. He brought up their many years of camaraderie and declared her friendship one that had helped shape him.

Then, he proposed.

CHAPTER TWENTY-THREE

Fezzi left and Belle returned to the drawing room, where her aunt and cousin were sitting beside one another on the settee, their backs to her. Aunt Agnes had her arm around Harriet and appeared to be comforting her. Harriet let out a soft sob.

Belle hesitated just past the doorway. Should she slip back out? Retire to her bedchamber for the night?

"There, there, dear," Aunt Agnes said in a low tone. "He's not the only man in the world."

The sight elicited so many emotions. Part of Belle wanted to reach out and hug Harriet as well; after all, Belle understood how it felt to be cast off by the man one had hoped would come up to scratch. A far less charitable side of Belle surged with triumph; Belle had a proposal while her self-serving cousin did not.

But the emotion that trumped all others was a deep sadness. The more attentively Belle watched the interaction, the more she could not help but think that if her own mother had lived, that might have been them. Her mother would have been reassurance and love when Belle was desolate and cold.

The realization of all that she'd lost made even her good news feel dim.

"Do you need something?" Aunt Agnes's question pulled Belle from her reverie.

In as few words as possible, Belle recounted her afternoon walk with Fezzi.

"You have accepted him then?" Aunt Agnes asked, her tone stiff.

Belle glanced at Harriet, who was decidedly not looking at Belle, before nodding. "Yes, I have accepted Lord Wilkins."

No one said a thing for a breath. Then Aunt Agnes pasted on a joyless smile. "We are happy for you, of course."

That was all. Both aunt and cousin turned their backs on Belle once more.

Belle's eyes filled with tears, forcing her to blink several times. Were they not going to say more than that? Could they not celebrate with her, even for an evening?

The fire in the hearth crackled as the log split in two, falling to either side. The waving shadows along the far wall drew Belle's attention. Even in shadow, it was evident that Aunt Agnes and Harriet cared for one another, and that they were determined to leave Belle out.

No more. She could not bear it. Spinning about, she hurried from the room. It was better to remove herself than make a scene, for she simply could not bear the rejection any longer. If only she could force the years-worth of memories such an image dredged up to leave her be, to haunt her no longer.

The next day, four days before Christmas Day, was no better. With Harriet despondent and complaining of a headache, Aunt Agnes refused Fezzi's offer to have them all over to Easthill Manor for dinner.

The day after that, Harriet kept to her room, as did Aunt Agnes. Belle, alone in an echoing stillness, was left to her own devices.

Two days before Christmas Day, Harriet spent every waking hour ordering Belle about. Belle was in her light and needed to move; Belle was hogging the cooked carrots and shouldn't stuff her mouth so full; Belle was flipping the pages of her book far too loudly.

When the sun dawned the following morning, Belle chose to simply remain in her room. She'd had enough. Christmas Eve or not, she was done with Harriet.

Partway through the morning, a knock sounded at her door. Praying desperately hard that it was not Harriet or Aunt Agnes coming to demand she join them, Belle moved to the door and opened it.

A footman stood on the other side. "This just arrived for you, miss," he said, holding out a small package.

"Oh, thank you," Belle said lamely, taking the box-shaped parcel from his hand.

The footman bowed and moved off.

Belle slowly shut the door, her gaze never leaving the package. It wasn't particularly heavy. She walked toward her bed. Nothing besides her name was written on it. It must have been hand delivered by a servant of the sender. Who could have possibly sent her something? Would Fezzi? Perhaps it was an engagement gift of some kind? Such would be sweet but didn't sound at all like the sort of thing Fezzi would do.

Belle sat atop her bed, holding the package in both her hands. She wanted desperately to open it, yet, inexplicably, she was hesitant.

No one had ever sent her a gift before. Her parents had gifted her a few things now and then, sometimes during Christmas, and once to celebrate her birthday. But since their passing, she hadn't received anything of note.

Lifting a hand, she gently pulled the brown paper away. Her breath caught.

A lovely, beautifully ornate box rested in her hand. It was

certainly the most elegant thing she'd ever owned. Carefully, she lifted the lid. Inside were four spools of handsome thread; forest green, maroon, primrose, and even dark blue, which was by far the hardest color to find and the most expensive.

She ran a finger over the spools. Who could have been so thoughtful? One of the spools shifted, showing a small bit of paper tucked beneath. Belle pulled it out and opened it.

The letter can never be allowed to hurt Fezzi. Meet me along the road at the edge of your Aunt's estate. Midnight tonight.

Please come,

—J

Good heavens, it was from James. He'd bought her thread. He'd remembered her commenting that she was nearly out; that moment when he'd happened upon her in Dunwell felt like a lifetime ago. So much had happened since then.

More than that, he wanted to see her again.

Of course, he only wanted her to help him make sure Fezzi's right to the earldom was never questioned. Did he want to see her for any other reason? They'd left things so wretchedly; did he want to set things right between them? Not a small part of her hoped so. She certainly did.

Belle shook her head. She was an engaged woman now; she ought not to be so concerned about a man who was not her betrothed. Still, after so many days of solitude and silence, she could not deny the warmth that came from the beautiful box and thread.

James was right. They needed to see that the letter was dealt with properly. She fingered the dark blue thread. James was one of the most thoughtful and selfless people she knew—gentleman or lady. He'd spent his entire time at Easthill Manor seeing to Fezzi's future. And for what? He gained nothing from protecting his cousin—

A sudden realization came crashing down upon her.

If Fezzi lost his title...it would go to James.

Belle sat, temporarily too stunned to move. Not only had James spent weeks looking after Fezzi, but he'd sacrificed his own comfort in the act. James could have very easily claimed the earldom as his right—it *was* his right to inherit. Instead, he'd protected Fezzi. Worked tirelessly to remove any evidence that might pose a threat.

A woman couldn't help but love a man like that.

Belle let out a soft sigh. Oh gracious, she *did* love him. She hadn't been aware of it only moments ago. Yet now, fingering the thread, holding the lovely box, and realizing all James had done for Fezzi as well as herself, Belle knew.

She loved James. Had *been* in love with James for weeks now.

Now that she knew, what on earth was she to do? She was engaged to Fezzi, after all. She'd already accepted him. Lady Wilkins knew. Her aunt and cousin knew. They all expected her to marry Fezzi; she'd expected as much from herself.

Not to mention, after all the horrid things she said to James last they spoke, she wouldn't blame him if he no longer cared to be near her.

Except—she lifted the small note once more—he had asked to see her. Still, the note gave no indication of how he was feeling toward her. Was he still angry? Did he see her as petty and self-serving? He had every right to feel that way if he did.

How she wanted to speak with him now, and not wait until tonight. But wait, she would have to do. After seeing James again, perhaps she would be able to sort out what she should do next.

CHAPTER TWENTY-FOUR

Would she meet him? James paced across the snow speckled grass. With only a bit of moonlight to keep him from falling on his face, he didn't go far before turning around once more and pacing back the way he'd come. Surely she would come.

The real question was which feeling possessed her most? Concern for Fezzi? Or anger toward him? James desperately wanted to see her again. Yet, if she did come, it meant her concern for Fezzi outweighed her feelings for *him*. Knowing as much didn't sit well. At the same time, if she didn't show, it meant she despised him. Either way, he and Belle would be at loggerheads.

She'd helped him so much this season. Indeed, she was the reason he'd found the blasted letter in the first place. If not for her, Fezzi would be in a much worse situation, though he'd never know it until it was too late. Belle, of all people, deserved to be present when he saw to Fezzi's future once and for all.

There was a soft crunch and James turned around.

Belle was dressed in a rich blue pelisse and a fur-trimmed hat with a matching muff. A touch of moonlight kissed her perfect lips and nose, but shadows hid her eyes. Her posture gave nothing away. She stood straight, her chin up. But that didn't tell him enough to know exactly where the two of them stood. Gads, but he hated himself for the things he'd said last time they spoke.

"You came," he said.

"I am as you see me." Her voice, like her posture, was neither overly cold nor expressly warm. It told him nothing regarding her current mood.

An ache to reach out and take hold of her gnawed at him. He coughed softly—if only he could dislodge the pang so easily—and strode to her side. "I was not sure how you would receive..."

"Your gift?"

James only nodded. Her tone had sounded a bit softer than before. Surely that was a good sign.

Belle walked up closer to him. "I was surprised. But...pleased."

Having Belle stand so close to him sent all reasonable ideas fleeing. He could hardly think straight. He certainly could not make heads nor tails of what she meant when she'd said *pleased*, nor could he understand the way her voice had lilted over the word.

"I have a sleigh just behind these trees." He forced the words out as he extended his arm. "Care to join me in seeing to it that Fezzi *remains* Lord Wilkins forever?"

The tips of her lovely pink lips turned up and she slipped her arm around his. "I think that sounds like the perfect way to spend a Christmas Eve."

Having her so near while not being at liberty to pull her in yet closer was like starving while sitting next to someone else who ate at their leisure, all the while unable to partake himself.

They walked in silence to the conveyance, and he handed

her up. It was only a small sleigh, but the roads were not terribly iced over just now.

Belle situated her skirts as James sat beside her.

"The heating block is lovely, thank you," she said.

Her sincere gratitude warmed his cheeks, though it was unwanted since he couldn't respond by slipping his arm around her shoulders, as he certainly wished to. Instead, James scooted as far away from her as he could manage and picked up the horses' reins. "I know the cold does not normally bother you, but it is an exceptionally chilly night, and I would hate for you to grow ill on my account." He called to the horses and they started forward.

The crackling of the sleigh runners breaking through the frost and piles of drifted snow along the road was all that was to be heard for quite some time. James found himself clenching the reins tightly. He and Belle had never passed so long a time in one another's presence with nothing to say. A comfortable silence was one thing—that they'd experienced together many a time. But this was certainly not such an experience. This was agonizing.

"Please," Belle finally whispered, "tell me that we aren't enemies."

Her soft plea nearly undid him. Turning toward her, he couldn't stop himself from pulling one of her hands out of the warm muff and holding it gently in his own. "No, my dear, never that."

"But you are upset with me." She didn't voice it as a question.

James let out a long breath. "Upset isn't the right word."

Beneath her bonnet, he could just barely make out her fretting over her lower lip. Gads, but she looked kissable.

"More than upset?" she asked.

He shook his head and faced the two horses once more, but he couldn't seem to make himself relinquish her hand. It felt entirely too perfect cupped inside his. "I was angry"—still was, truth be told—"but not *at* you."

"At what, then?"

At Fezzi; at his stupidity for waiting so long to claim Belle's hand that James had fallen for his beautiful bride-to-be in the interim; at the whole deuced situation. Struggling to put it all in words, he only squeezed her hand.

She seemed to understand, for she nodded and turned to face the horses as well. More than that, Belle seemed to relax beside him. It was still vastly different from the ease they'd conversed with in the past, but it was better than it had been only a few minutes ago.

"I am sorry," she said.

He took to rubbing the back of her hand with his thumb. He couldn't force himself to let go, but if he didn't do something to distract himself, he was liable to pull her into an embrace.

"I do understand, you know," he said, even as the trees around them made way for dark buildings. "For a man, title and wealth are everything. It changes how people see you, how they treat you. It changes the opportunities you are given, and the opportunities your children will be given." He glanced her way. "I can only imagine how it would be even more true for a woman."

Belle didn't respond to that, though she did not pull her hand away; he took that as a good sign.

He turned the horses, directing them to pull up along the side of the road. "We're here," he announced.

Belle's head tipped up. "I thought we were going to Easthill Manor."

James stood. "No. Besides you and me, there are only a few others who know of this letter. One, in particular, I wanted to be sure understood my decision to bury the past in no uncertain terms." He stepped down and secured the horses.

Belle scooted to the edge of the bench seat, where he'd been sitting only moments ago. As James moved back toward the sleigh, he found himself at eye level with her.

"Thank you," Belle said with a smile. "Fezzi may be forever ignorant, but on his behalf, I think you should know that you're doing a very noble thing."

"It is nothing more than he would do for me if the roles were reversed. Though I must admit, hearing you question if I *would* do the right thing was rather a painful moment." He meant it as a lighthearted tease, but it left his lips with far too much sincerity for that. Having missed his jesting mark, he met her gaze and conceded the last bit—the part that had been eating at him for days now. "I would have thought you trusted me more than that."

Reaching out, Belle placed a gloved hand against one side of his face. The hand still surrounded by the muff she placed against the other side, fur and all.

"Of course I trust you," she said. Then her lip quirked upward in far too saucy an expression. "If you need proof, only look around. Do you think I'd agree to a midnight ride, *alone*, with just any gentleman?"

"Do not worry," he said, leaning in a bit despite his better judgment. "We'll bury tonight along with the letter. Your reputation is safe with me."

"I know." She said the words with full confidence. James felt his resolve to remain only friends weaken. "I do trust you, James. I am sorry if my actions led you to believe otherwise."

"After the things I said, I would not blame you for never speaking to me again."

"And what did you say that I did not deserve?"

James let out a dark chuckle. "All of it. I've been most grievously sorry for the things I said last we spoke."

She watched him, a sad sort of hope in her eyes. Her look drew out his next whispered words. "You have no idea how sorry I've been." It would be so easy to kiss her again. Her hands still held him close, her lips only a few centimeters away.

But no. Not only would it be a horrid misstep—again—there was something far more important. Placing his hands on either side of her waist, he lifted her down from the sleigh. Even when her feet hit the ground, he didn't let go.

"Miss Belle Young, I have something I need to say to you, and I need you to listen right proper."

Her eyes were wide, but she only nodded.

Gads, she was every bit as lovely surprised as she was angry. Or teasing. Or fretting away at her lovely bottom lip.

"I came across you and Lady Wilkins here in town a few weeks ago. You were speaking with a footman's niece, one you knew by name."

Belle nodded again, confusion etching itself deeper into her brow the more he spoke.

"Then the morning after Lady Wilkins's headache"—it was safer than saying "the morning after we kissed," though that would be forever how he thought of it—"you spoke to a different footman before sitting down to breakfast. Again, you knew of his individual circumstance. You knew enough of the tenants and servants at Easthill Manor to make each Christmas box unique. I would wager you know more about Mrs. Byrd than even Lady Wilkins."

He kept his hands around her waist, hoping she would come to see what he desperately needed her to understand. "Why is that?" he asked, not because *he* needed to know the answer—he already knew—but because he needed *her* to know.

Belle glanced about, working her lower lip. After a minute of silence, she calmed and placed her hands on either one of his arms.

"They are people," she said, "just like you and me. They love and they hurt. They dream and they work. They may not have as many nice things, and their heritage may not include dukes and earls but"—she gave a little shrug—"they still matter to someone. They're still parents and sons and daughters; they're husbands and wives, brothers and sisters."

He gave her a gentle shake. "And the fact that they don't have titles or wealth doesn't change that."

Belle's gaze dropped to his chest, and James got the distinct impression she didn't wish to meet his eyes. He pressed on regardless.

"*You*, too, matter. You are a daughter, a cousin, a niece. You love and hurt, dream and work."

Moonlight glinted off a tear running down her cheek. James thumbed it away, then hooked a finger under her chin and lifted her eyes to his. "I'll not stand between you and Fezzi. It is your life, and you must decide what is best for you. But, please, you have to understand that you don't need a title or wealth. Belle, you matter, and you always will."

She blinked several times, sending more tears down her cheeks, but she smiled all the same.

Her eyes were far too mesmerizing for either of their good, even moist as they were now.

James released her and leaned back. "That's all I wanted to say." He took her hand and looped it around his arm. "Now come; we should see to making sure Fezzi never has to leave Easthill Manor unless he wishes it himself."

CHAPTER TWENTY-FIVE

Belle could barely stand. If not for her hand looped around James's arm she more likely than not would have found herself on the icy ground.

You matter, and you always will, he'd said. Belle shook her head and wiped a hand over her wet cheek. No one had ever said anything half so sweet to her.

More than that, she found part of her actually believed him. When he'd spoken of her having dreams and hurt, same as those around her, it had been as though something had clicked inside her head. Something had firmed up, something had ignited.

Was he right?

What would that be like to innately believe one's self had value? Apart from titles and wealth and the gossip of society?

James rapped heavily against an old wooden door, drawing Belle's mind back to the present. Slits of candlelight shone through cracks in the door.

She'd felt like that door so many times. Very nearly what she ought to be, but too broken, too imperfect to truly be right.

But James clearly didn't see her that way.

So which was right?

Was she the broken door, or a valuable lady?

The door swung open, and an elderly man with white hair framing an enlarging bald spot ushered them in.

"Mr. Radcliff," the elderly man said, remarkably cheerful for such a late evening. "You have only just missed Mr. Marley."

"I am sorry to hear it," James said. "I understood Mr. Scrooge was to be working late tonight?"

The elderly man bowed. "All too true, I'm afraid."

Belle lifted an eyebrow in question. Who worked this late on Christmas Eve?

James caught sight of her expression and only shrugged.

With a wave of a hand, the elderly man showed them into a small room off to their right. Another man, whom Belle assumed must be Mr. Scrooge, sat behind a faded desk that looked as worn out as the door.

After introducing Belle to the man—she was right in thinking he was Mr. Scrooge—James added, "Thank you for being willing to meet with me on such short notice."

Mr. Scrooge pointed them toward a couple of seats across from his desk. "Not all of us have the privilege of taking time off every twenty-fourth of December."

Dear me, he was a stingy old man.

For his part, James seemed to have anticipated such a response. "And none are more appreciative of your commitment to your work than I, at least for tonight."

Mr. Scrooge went so far as to have the audacity to guffaw at James's words. "Have you found the letter, then?"

"Miss Young did," James said as he slipped something from his jacket pocket.

Belle caught no more than a passing glimpse as James handed the folded paper over to Mr. Scrooge. But that was all it took for her to identify it as the letter she'd found in the den. The look of it was forever emblazoned on her mind.

Mr. Scrooge took it from James and opened it without another word. His gaze moved across the paper. Tension wrapped itself securely around Belle's throat. Suppose this man could not be trusted? Suppose he made the contents of this letter known to all? He could ruin Fezzi.

Belle glanced over at James. Was he quite sure about this course of action? But James's expression was not one of worry over what Mr. Scrooge might do, but one determined to see his plan through. Those beautiful, expressive blue eyes told her that James indeed trusted this man. Grouch though he may be, James had seen fit to bring this matter to him.

If James trusted Mr. Scrooge with this, then Belle could trust James and not fret so.

A small voice in her head couldn't help but wonder. If Belle trusted James's opinion of Mr. Scrooge, shouldn't she also trust James's opinion of herself? Belle could not deny that if James introduced her to any individual—gentleman or lady—and said that this person was wise and trustworthy, Belle would believe him. Yet, when he'd said similar things about her, she struggled.

Still, even now as she remembered his words, the way he'd focused so intently on her, she *did* feel herself believing what he'd said.

"How do you wish to proceed, Mr. Radcliff?" Mr. Scrooge said, folding up the letter once more.

"Are you certain that, provided we destroy this letter, Fezzi's claim to the Wilkins title will be secure?"

"Yes," Mr. Scrooge said. "With Mr. Thrup no longer with us, this letter alone could cause your cousin alarm." He tossed it onto his desk. "Truthfully, with the biological father dead, even this may not be enough. Still, if you wish to claim yourself as the rightful heir, we can try."

Belle was struck again with how selfless James was acting. Was it any wonder she'd fallen in love with him? It seemed, too, that he had forgiven her. She was not fully sure what she was to do next, but hope was once more blossoming inside her.

James shook his head. "You've known from the beginning that wasn't my design."

Mr. Scrooge, for his part, turned pointedly toward Belle. "Perhaps you would have better luck than I, miss," he said, addressing her. "It's no sin to want to look out for one's self. If my life in this forlorn world has shown me anything, it's that every man must fend for himself. There is never any reason to expect another's aid when it is most needed."

"It sounds, sir," Belle replied, sitting up straighter, "that you have had a rather dreary existence."

"And if I have?" His voice grew in volume.

Belle probably would have cowed before such a gruff statement not six weeks ago. Now, though, with James's words taking root inside her, she found she could sit, unflinching. "Then I am sorry for it."

"Bah," he all but barked.

"Sir," James said, a hint of warning in his tone, "you will remember you are addressing a lady."

Mr. Scrooge didn't say more, but neither did he continue to scowl quite so meanly.

James stood, picking up the letter, and walked to the hearth where a small fire burned low. "After tonight," he said, speaking more to Mr. Scrooge than her, "we, none of us, will ever breathe word of this again. Is that clear?"

Mr. Scrooge's face deepened into a hard grimace, but he nodded.

James tossed the letter into the fire. Old and dry, it burned quickly, the edges turning black and then disappearing in flames. A peace settled around Belle as she watched that lonely bit of evidence turn to ash. Fezzi was safe. His mother was safe, too.

A small part of her realized this meant her own claim to the title of Lady Wilkins was also safe, yet the thought didn't warm her as the other realizations had.

Nonetheless, knowing that Fezzi and Lady Wilkins were secure in Easthill Manor *did* warm her. Her gaze lifted to James, still standing by the hearth. The soft smile across his face told her that he felt the same.

They'd done it. They'd protected Fezzi.

"Thank you, sir." James spoke to Mr. Scrooge even as he moved over to Belle and offered a hand to help her rise. "The information and connections you have provided me have been most appreciated."

"Still say you're acting a deuced fool," Mr. Scrooge said, shaking his head.

"Here we are, all the same," James said. He tucked Belle's hand beneath his arm. "Come, Belle. We best be on our way."

She nodded her agreement. She was overjoyed at what they had done that night, but she had no desire to stay in Mr. Scrooge's company one minute longer.

"Belle?" Mr. Scrooge spoke in a slightly strangled voice.

Both she and James turned, looking at him once more.

Mr. Scrooge had stopped halfway up from rising from his chair. He peered at her, something very different crossing his expression. Unfocused thought, perhaps? Or a fond, yet painful memory?

"I knew a Belle once," he said. By the tone of his voice, his Belle had meant something dear to him.

"Oh?" Belle pressed softly.

But Mr. Scrooge's expression only hardened once again. "She, too, pressured me to make unwise financial decisions." His hard stare turned toward James. "You would do well to heed my warning. Women will claim to love you, but the moment you apply yourself to being prosperous or industrious they will claim you have grown greedy." His gaze returned to Belle even as he seemed to continue to speak to James. "They will say you've taken leave of all your nobler pursuits."

Belle felt suddenly cold. Mr. Scrooge's words were a most uncomfortable echo of what James had said to her not long ago. He'd claimed she'd given up what made her most lovely—her interest in the servants around her, her willingness to see them as people with lives, even her puppet show—all in the pursuit of title and wealth.

Was she like Mr. Scrooge? Was *that* what she was allowing herself to become?

"Mr. Scrooge." James's tone was far more threatening now.

Belle stilled him with a hand on his arm. She had no desire to become even remotely like Mr. Scrooge, with his hard scowls and embittered tone, but she could not deny that, in some respects, she understood him.

"You say, sir," Belle said in an even, firm tone, "that your life has shown you there is never any hope of another's aid. I understand that feeling. It can leave one to think they must abandon all for the security that money provides."

Mr. Scrooge did not seem pleased with her words. "Don't flatter yourself thinking you know me." Slowly he walked around from behind the beaten desk. "Do you know why I am still at work on Christmas Eve? It is because I've *always* worked on Christmas Eve. My family sent me away to a boarding school the very moment I was old enough to be accepted. They left me there, year after year, not even willing to see me over the Christmas holidays. I learned as a child, Miss Young, that hope was a fruitless endeavor."

"I can relate to being left behind during the festive season," she said. "I know what it is like to feel as though your life is controlled by another. That this other person has the power to make you happy or unhappy." She'd often seen Aunt Agnes in that light, at first, and then Fezzi. They had means and connections, and she'd felt desperate for their approval.

The strange thing was, she was beginning to think that perhaps she no longer did.

"But," Belle continued, "I cannot agree that hope is a fruitless endeavor."

"Oh?" Mr. Scrooge said, the bite in his tone less harsh. "I suppose your 'other person' used their power to make you happy then? So you do not understand me after all."

"No," Belle answered honestly, thinking of Aunt Agnes. "And so I placed my hope in another."

Mr. Scrooge's gaze jumped to James, probably assuming she meant him.

And there was the rub. She *hadn't* placed her hope in James; she'd never seen him as the one who would take her away from her miserable life at Wilmington Bury. Yet he was the one who had made her happy—the happiest she'd ever been.

"No," Belle repeated yet again. "And only now I am realizing that I had it all wrong to begin with." She took a step closer to Mr. Scrooge, wishing she could somehow reach out to him in such a way that he would understand *her* and all she was now coming to recognize. "We do not engage in a fruitless endeavor when we hope; we engage in a fruitless endeavor when we place that hope in *someone else*. When we say that another person has the power to make us happy or unhappy, we give up all responsibility for our *own* happiness."

"If not in someone else, then in who do we hope?" he asked.

"In God and in ourselves."

"You see yourself as divine as that? To place yourself next to Him?"

"No, certainly not." Quite the opposite in fact. "What I mean is maybe we should place hope in our own ability to learn from hardship, our capacity to grow into wiser and better individuals despite all the heartache. And then, place hope in His strength to guide us beyond the pain and to help us find another happy life."

He watched her, his gaze intently focused on her face. She felt sure he was truly hearing her. Then, in a blink, he shook his head and his scowl returned.

"Humbug," he grumbled, returning to his seat behind the desk.

James's hand rested against her arm, tugging her softly toward the door. Belle nodded her agreement; it was time to leave. She'd tried, but it seemed Mr. Scrooge was not yet ready to change.

The elderly man who'd opened the door to them earlier appeared at their side. "Forgive him," he said in a soft voice, probably wishing Mr. Scrooge would not over hear. "He's had a touch of fever these past few days. I'm afraid he's not quite himself just now." His voice grew distant as he spoke, as though he were thinking to himself. "Perhaps I should summon my grand-daughter. She would know what to do. She always knows what to do."

"It is not a fever," Mr. Scrooge said, his head still bent down over some papers across his desk. "It is only a slight disorder of the stomach brought on, no doubt, by an undigested bit of beef, a blot of mustard, or crumb of cheese, a fragment of an underdone potato."

"But, sir—"

"I have only just rid myself of one dreadful business, and with my niece harassing me day and night I have yet another to go. Summon your granddaughter and my future shall be as bleak as my past and present."

The elderly man only shook his head as if to say, *what do you do with such a man?* Then he opened the door for James and Belle. James stepped out, but before Belle did, she turned one last time and looked over at Mr. Scrooge. His eyes had wandered away from his paperwork, his gaze unfocused and hazy. His cantankerous air seemed to float away for a moment and in the light of the candle atop his desk, he looked to be little more than a sad, lonely man.

In a blink, his face hardened once more. Taking hold of an extinguisher cap and with a sudden action, he pressed it down upon the candle. For a brief moment light continued to stream out from under the cap, an unbroken ring atop the table. Then, it snuffed out the light and the room grew slightly darker.

Belle's lips turned down at the sight. Perhaps if Mr. Scrooge took the time to mull over her words, he would finally hear what she'd said. Perhaps he only needed a bit more time.

Belle moved out into the night, and the door shut fully behind them.

James's arms moved around her, holding her in a warm hug. "You should have seen yourself just now. Anyone privileged enough to witness that would never doubt of your beauty and wisdom."

She shouldn't have done it, but Belle wrapped her arms around James in return. "What you did tonight was every bit as wondrous."

Tomorrow she would be at Wilmington Bury and he at Easthill Manor, quite far away from each other. It was better that way. Still, she felt strangely elated. It was no doubt a mixture of James's words to her earlier and her own revelation which came while speaking with Mr. Scrooge. She would allow herself this one moment, and this one moment only.

"I thought about waiting until tomorrow," James said, not appearing to wish the closeness between them to stop. "Then I could say it was a Christmas Day present, but once I'd decided on this course of action, I felt I couldn't wait even the extra twelve hours."

Belle felt a yawn come on, one she couldn't suppress. "I'm not sure it still is Christmas Eve."

James, keeping one arm around her, pulled a pocket watch out. Angling it back, he caught a bit of light coming from the broken slats in the door.

Belle leaned over as well. "There, see? It is one in the morning. Of a certain, it is now Christmas Day."

James chuckled softly. "I suppose I had been looking for a Christmas gift for Lady Wilkins all along."

"Truly," Belle said, as they slowly made their way back to the sleigh, "this is the best Christmas gift you could have given her, even if she'll never know of it."

CHAPTER TWENTY-SIX

*J*ames awoke late on Boxing Day. He'd been quite happy all the day before, Christmas Day, if a bit exhausted. After retiring early, he'd expected to awake closer to his normal time. Apparently, his late-night Christmas Eve was still hanging about him.

He readied for the day quickly. Once dressed, James made his way out of his room and toward the den. Fezzi would probably be in there. Not only had James been tired the previous day, he'd also been cantankerous. Everyone had noticed it. Lady Wilkins hadn't said anything, but she'd given him a questioning eye more than once. The Smiths had all steered clear of him; even sweet Miss Nancy had avoided his company. Fezzi had finally called him out on it after the ladies had left them to port after dinner.

But what could James say? *Thanks for stepping up and being a true gentleman like I repeatedly told you to do, but now I'd really rather marry Belle myself. You see, last night she showed me what an insightful, understanding, wise woman she truly is, and I don't think I can live without her.*

It would have been true. But also very wrong to say.

So he'd retired early.

Movement outside caught his eye, and James walked over to a tall, narrow window along the wall. It looked out toward the front of the manor. There, Fezzi stood, Belle beside him next to a sleigh full of boxes to be passed out to tenants.

He could see little more than the top of her bonnet and the way her skirts swirled around her as she turned to speak with one of the footmen.

Blast, but she *was* everything he wanted. There was a very real chance he *couldn't* live without her. But she was engaged to Fezzi now. Her hopes from Christmases past had finally come true. He'd meant it when he'd said he wouldn't stand in her way.

He wouldn't.

But neither could he stay here and watch them wed.

Pushing off the window, he stalked back toward his bedchamber. He'd only come to Easthill Manor for one reason this winter—to save Fezzi.

Now, he'd done just that. Fezzi was heir to the Wilkins title, and nothing and no one could take that away from him any longer.

Now that Fezzi's future was seen to, it would be best if James started seeing to his own future.

He would start with a prompt removal from Easthill Manor, and he would stay away for good.

BELLE SAT STRAIGHT, HER BACK A RIGID POLE. HARRIET SAT across from her, and Aunt Agnes was to her left. Thankfully, Fezzi was on her right. If not for his nearness, she might not have enjoyed the evening meal at all. Still, even the sight of the yule log burning in the hearth and the smell of evergreen boughs did very little to brighten the room. At least for Belle,

Easthill Manor no longer felt warm and inviting. Somehow it had stopped being home.

She knew why. James had left.

He'd quit the county, and he hadn't even said goodbye.

Blinking several times, Belle dropped her gaze to the soup before her. She'd thought back so many times to Christmas Eve, to hers and James's midnight adventure. She'd thought, then, that perhaps there was a chance that they might make a match. That he might love her even. Even just the thought sent her heart racing and her cheeks to the blush.

But Christmas had been four days ago. And now, James was gone. She'd learned as much from Fezzi. Why hadn't James told her himself? Did he not even care enough to let her know that he was leaving?

Belle picked up her glass and took a small sip. She wasn't at all sure what was in the glass or if it was fine or bitter. Neither did she care.

Though she and Fezzi had been engaged over a week, tonight was the first time Aunt Agnes had accepted Fezzi's daily invitation to dinner. With Belle's aunt still believing the families were to be joined soon, she couldn't fathom why Aunt Agnes had postponed becoming more familiar with Fezzi and Lady Wilkins. She suspected it had to do with Harriet's disappointment only a week ago and her cousin's unwillingness to go out in society.

Belle had at first been happy to hear they were finally going to Easthill Manor for an evening but had been struggling to find the right topics of conversation ever since they'd arrived. Blessedly, Mrs. Smith and Lady Wilkins had done a fine job filling the table with talk. Miss Smith, Belle noticed with not a small twinge of guilt, was unusually silent.

Finally, the meal ended, and the ladies rose from the table. The two matrons led the way back to the drawing room. Miss Smith and her two young sisters followed close behind. Several steps back, Belle and Harriet trailed after them.

"Rather high in the instep now, aren't you?" Harriet said, taking hold of Belle's arm and not allowing her the chance to escape. "You have your earl, after all. I must admit, to my surprise. I had not thought you capable of catching a gentleman of the *haut ton*."

Belle bit her lip for a moment. There had been a time when she would have accepted such criticism, even believed it. But since Christmas Eve, everything had begun to change. Then, on the Holyday itself, while traveling to church, she'd happened to cross paths with Mr. Scrooge once more. She'd been shocked at the sight of him; he'd seemed a changed man. Their short conversation had baffled her, but he clearly had been appreciative of all she'd said the previous night. Perhaps she *had* stumbled across something there in his office. Something that might prove useful now.

Instead of capitulating to her cousin's harsh appraisal, Belle stopped walking and, in the middle of the corridor, faced Harriet fully. "I want you to know," Belle said sincerely, "that I am sorry things did not work out between you and His Grace. But you should also know that not all hope is lost."

To her surprise, Harriet's eyes shone with unshed tears. "That's easy enough for you to say. You've secured your own future."

It was easy to understand Harriet's bitterness. It was naturally easy to downplay another's uncertainty from a position of assumed security.

"Regardless," Belle said, "it doesn't change your situation. You are still beautiful, and you still have many opportunities before you. Learn what you can from this Christmas; let it mold you into a kinder, more understanding woman. Then, very soon, I'm sure, the right gentleman will come along and be unable to resist you."

The smallest hint of a smile tugged at Harriet's lips. "Perhaps." Slipping her arm away from Belle's, she continued down the corridor and toward the drawing room.

Belle watched her leave but did not follow. Maybe, like Mr. Scrooge, with some time, Harriet would understand.

She tipped her head back and looked toward the high ceiling. The grand archways above her, the elegant decorations around her, and the well-kept floors beneath her feet had all felt like home not that long ago. Now, though, it no longer did.

James had come and taken her heart, and when he'd left, he'd taken her feeling of home with him.

It was time she faced up to that truth. It was time to say goodbye to Easthill Manor. Goodbye to all she'd held on to for so very long.

Heavy footsteps echoed behind her. Belle turned to find Mr. Smith and Fezzi walking her way.

For days now, ever since her last conversation with James, she'd been looking for the right time to speak with Fezzi. Nothing had presented itself, however. If the right time was not going to find Belle, she would find it instead.

She offered a quick curtsy to both gentlemen when they neared her. "Fezzi, might I have a word with you?"

"Of course," Fezzi said, his words slightly drawn out. Mr. Smith excused himself and continued on his way to the drawing room.

The wariness on his face clearly indicated that Fezzi was at a loss as to why she wished to speak to him now, after they'd spent all of Boxing Day delivering packages together and a full dinner, besides. But there had always been other people about. Now, she finally had him alone.

"Is something wrong?" Fezzi began.

"Yes," Belle said. It was all she could get out before having to draw herself up and reaffirm that this was the right course of action. "I have been thinking...a lot, as of late."

"All right."

Belle pursed her lips momentarily. This sudden wave of shyness was ridiculous. This was Fezzi she was speaking to. The man who had befriended her when there had been no one else around.

"I wish to speak plainly," she said.

"By all means."

Poor man; he looked so very confused. "What I mean to say is this. For several days now I have been thinking this over, so I don't want you to feel I have rushed to this decision or that I don't know my own mind on this account."

His confusion now looked to have taken on a hint of wariness as well.

"Fezzi," Belle pressed on, "I want you to know that your friendship will always be most dear to me. You showed me joy and happiness when I lived in almost constant gloom. You are a good man and have proven yourself to be an honorable one as well. However, I wish to end our engagement."

His jaw dropped. For a moment, Belle wondered if he wouldn't topple over as well. Instead, he only shook himself and said, "I can only assume this is in part due to Miss Smith."

Belle nodded.

"But you must know," he said, "that after we are married, I promise to be always faithful. I would never—"

"Oh, Fezzi." Belle almost laughed as she cupped his face in her hands. "I know, someday soon, you will be a very faithful husband. Just not mine."

"I don't understand."

"I care greatly for you Fezzi, and I always will. But I'm not in love with you, and you aren't in love with me."

He silently shrugged, no doubt not seeing why that changed matters. Many of his acquaintances had likely married for convenience.

Her hands dropped away from his face, resting against his

shoulders. How could she help him understand? "I'm releasing you from your promise."

"Why?"

"It was wrong of me to pressure you into a connection from the beginning."

"But I'd given you my word."

Truly? He was still fighting her on this. "I thought you would be happy; you are free now."

"You are in earnest?"

What did it take to convince him? "Yes. I'll write down my decision and sign my name to the bottom if that makes you feel better."

A smile finally broke out across his face. He slipped his arms around her waist and hugged her tightly. "Thank you," he whispered.

Belle hugged him back but couldn't deny that hugging Fezzi was what she'd always imagined hugging a brother would feel like. James's embrace was a sharp contrast to this one.

The soft pad of slippered feet against the hard floor drew both their attention toward the far side of the hall. Miss Smith had slipped from the drawing room and was quickly making her way toward the staircase, her head determinedly down.

Fezzi glanced at Belle, a question in his brow.

"Go." She urged him forward.

With a parting smile, Fezzi jogged toward the staircase. "Miss Smith?" he called.

She didn't turn or glance his way but continued her flight up the stairs.

"George."

At her given name, she stilled.

It seemed the time had come for Belle to be the one to keep her head determinedly down. She moved past them quickly, wishing to give them as much privacy as she could. Still, she overheard their whispered conversation. As Belle reached the drawing room doors, she glanced back.

Fezzi had his arms wrapped around Miss Smith and their shared kiss made Belle blush. It also made her ache for James. How she wished he was still here.

But here or not, she did not regret her actions. James had reminded her that it was better to hope than to settle. She was better off loving herself, instead of playing society's games and trying to prove she deserved its fickle love.

With a sigh she kept to herself, Belle looked away. She had not released Fezzi with the misguided notion that now James would materialize at Easthill Manor. He had left without so much as a farewell, and she had no idea where he was. Nonetheless, Belle was decided. She would not stop Fezzi and Miss Smith from loving one another. Instead, she would place her own hope in a new life, one in which she was a kinder, more understanding woman. One in which she valued herself, despite her father's lack of title or wealth.

Belle stepped into the drawing room. Though she was very happy for Fezzi and Miss Smith, the time had come for her to claim a headache. With any luck, she could urge her aunt and cousin home before Fezzi and Miss Smith announced their happy news to their parents.

Despite Belle's role in this turn of events, she was not the least bit eager to be among company when her broken engagement became known to all.

Though, perhaps before she departed, she might misplace a few books for Mrs. Byrd to find. It would be her farewell present to Easthill Manor. A sort of thank you for all the acceptance, love, and gentle lessons it had given her through the years.

CHAPTER TWENTY-SEVEN

*J*ames leaned back and the chair beneath him groaned. The din of heavy voices filled the pub; somewhere on the other side of the large public dining room, the soft strains of a fiddle rounded out the bustle of the room. The man played *Greensleeves*— the very song he and Belle had danced to that wondrous and cursed night.

James picked up his tin mug, but only stared down at its contents instead of draining it. Someday, if there was any mercy in this life, he would forget what he'd felt that night. He'd forget the feel of her arms around him, of her fingers curling through his hair. He'd forget the easy way they laughed together and the jokes they'd shared. He'd forget the all-consuming feel of her lips against his.

He slammed the mug back onto the circular, wooden table.

Someday he *would* forget.

He had to; remembering was driving him mad.

"There's a very good chance he has continued on."

James glanced up. That masculine voice was far too familiar to ignore.

"We will check all the pubs in this town first," a brisk female voice replied, "and if he isn't here then we'll check the next town."

James slowly stood. It couldn't be.

"Very well, my love," the man replied.

James turned around.

Surely it wasn't...but it was. Fezzi and Miss Smith stood near the pub front door, both dressed in heavy coats and warm hats. Their eyes roamed about the large space, clearly looking for someone.

Looking for him, perhaps?

If both Fezzi and Miss Smith were here, was Belle with them? He stared at the two, though they clearly had not seen him among the mass of humanity. Part of him wished to rush over and greet his two good friends. Another part of him wasn't sure what he'd do if Belle turned out to be among them. He was equally unsure what he'd do if she *hadn't* accompanied them.

Though he looked over every individual most carefully, James did not see Belle at all.

That meant when Fezzi had said "my love," he had been referring to Miss Smith. What in thunderation was his cousin about this time? James knew full well that Fezzi had proposed to Belle, and she'd accepted him. If Fezzi was trying to wriggle his way out of his obligation *now*, he would find James more than simply opposed to the notion.

Miss Smith spotted him, her eyes clearing the moment her gaze landed on his face. He'd been found and recognized. There was no avoiding the encounter now.

She placed a hand on Fezzi's arm and all but dragged James's cousin over to him.

"There you are," Miss Smith said by way of greeting. "Good heavens, would it have been too much to ask to choose a less out-of-the way pub to dine in?" Her eyes moved from him to the dirty floors beneath their feet and then on to the ruckus that was taking place behind James. "Or at least one less...public?"

What were they doing here? James glanced over at Fezzi, but his cousin seemed equally disinclined to clarify.

"Good evening to you both," James said, his words dragged out. Whatever these two had come for, he wasn't interested in prolonging the conversation.

Fezzi smiled a deeply happy smile. "We wanted you to be one of the first to know; we are to be congratulated."

Judging by his tone and wide grin, Fezzi expected James to laugh and cheer and generally be merry that the two were engaged. But James only felt his expression grow darker. "What of Belle?" he asked.

Fezzi shrugged, "She cried off."

That was it? Belle had called off her engagement to Fezzi? She'd been hoping for such a connection for years; she wouldn't just cry off for no reason. His gaze jumped from Fezzi to Miss Smith, taking in the way they looked longingly at one another and the subtle way they leaned toward the other. Of course, Belle could have been made to feel she ought to cry off. Belle was too kindhearted by half.

"And why, pray tell,"—James's tone sounded menacing even in his own ears—"did Belle feel compelled to cry off?"

Fezzi had the audacity to shrug again. "Not sure. She said something about not wanting to pressure me into a connection and that she wasn't *in* love with me, therefore..." He let the rest of the sentence dangle.

"She was worried about pressuring *you*?" Fezzi—who in every respect should be the one to come up to scratch and see to Belle's happiness? After all he'd promised her and all the trust she'd put in him? All the hope she'd centered on him?

James opened and closed his fist. "If I learn that you've twisted her arm—"

"Fezzi, dear," Miss Smith interrupted, placing a hand on Fezzi's chest. "Do go see to some refreshments, please. Now that we've found James at last, I find I am quite famished."

"Right away, my sweet," Fezzi said, though his eyes didn't leave James. He appeared perplexed by James's evident anger, the nodcock. Without another word, Fezzi strolled away to find the establishment's landlord.

"Sit with me, if you please."

James glanced over, only to find that Miss Smith had seated herself at his table. His jaw ground tight, but he sat all the same.

He knew the look on his face clearly showed how he was feeling, but one look at it and Miss Smith only smiled the brighter.

"No doubt," she said with something bordering a laugh, "you are quite put out with Fezzi and me at the moment."

Put out was nowhere near a strong enough word, though he gathered that Miss Smith knew as much. "I would like a clear explanation, yes," he said.

Miss Smith's smile faded. Though she still held herself straight and with poise, he sensed her sincerity. "I will not deny that when I learned of Fezzi's previous promise to Miss Young, and then of their engagement, I, too, was *put out*." She placed her hands on the table, her white kid gloves standing out in stark contrast to the dark wood. "I was miserable. Then, four days after Christmas, Miss Young joined us for a family dinner. The ladies retired to the drawing room while the men stayed behind for port, only Miss Young didn't follow. Well, she did at first, but she stayed behind, in the corridor, waiting for the men. I was...trying to not appear upset, but I was failing miserably. So I excused myself early. As I headed toward my bedchamber, I spotted Miss Young and Fezzi in an embrace." Her cheeks heated, and she refused to look at him. "I nearly began to cry. I wanted nothing more than to slip upstairs unseen."

Could she not get to the point any quicker than this? Still, this was Miss Smith speaking; she seemed to never say in two sentences what she reasonably could stretch into ten. James waited, letting her tell the tale in her own way.

"Fezzi called to me. I stopped and waited, expecting him to simply inquire why I was retiring so early. Except," her tone took on a lighter, joyful lilt, "that wasn't it at all. He didn't say much, only that Miss Young had released him from his promise. That he was free to—that *we* were free to marry." Her face lit up; like the bright fire of a yuletide log, she glowed. "I cannot tell you how overjoyed I was."

"So it was Fezzi who pressured Belle into letting him go?" He believed Fezzi to have more honor than this. James should have stayed at Easthill Manor, stayed and made sure Fezzi *followed through* on his word.

Miss Smith reached out and placed a hand on his arm. "The next morning, I began to worry over the same." She pulled back but faced him this time, her gaze not leaving his. "Without Fezzi's knowledge, I called on Miss Young that very morning. I needed to know that she was all right. She's become such a dear friend to me, I couldn't bear the thought of my happiness coming at her sorrow."

The sincerity in Miss Smith's voice calmed some of the anger boiling inside him. Her tale may yet prove Fezzi to be an addle-minded ninnyhammer, but at least he knew Miss Smith was not a cruel supplanter.

"She convinced me that her releasing Fezzi was an act of her own will, stating that neither he nor I had done anything wrong. She spoke on, saying something about hope, how the best kind of hope was not a rigid belief that one's dream must come true in the fashion one first envisions, but that hope is trusting we can all learn and become better no matter what befalls us. The best kind of hope is believing, even when the thing we hoped for does not materialize, that God has something else, equally as good, in store."

Furious though he still was, James could not help but smile. Gads, but that sounded just like his Belle, insightful and kind. Had she not said nearly the same thing on Christmas Eve to Mr. Scrooge?

Fezzi returned with a barman directly behind him, carrying a tray of bread and cold cuts. As Fezzi sat and they began eating, the conversation naturally flowed to other things—Lady Wilkins's health, the upcoming Twelfth Night ball, the unexpectedly warm weather, and other equally unimportant things.

James though, found it hard to focus on any one topic for long. Not until, once the food had been cleared, Miss Smith grabbed his attention fully when she said, "Gather your bags, Mr. Radcliff. You are returning to Easthill Manor with us."

"Pardon me?" he asked her.

Fezzi looked at Miss Smith, his expression showing as much surprise as James felt. "I thought we were only here to share the good news with James," Fezzi said. "He has plenty of time to see to the matters of his estate and still return for the wedding."

The look Miss Smith gave Fezzi was exquisite. It was one part undying love, and one part "dear, you're an idiot." But all she said was, "I realize that, my love, but I am sure Mr. Radcliff does not want to miss Miss Young's puppet show."

She'd canceled that though. "Is she doing one after all?"

Fezzi pulled his lips to one side. "Yesterday she asked if I would allow her to put it on, and I agreed. Though I don't see how she'll pull it off. Her aunt has forbidden her to come anywhere near Easthill Manor. She claimed the children will be disappointed, so I gave my permission anyway. Truthfully, I think she plans to sneak in the servants' door, put on the show, and slip out before anyone is the wiser."

James's chest warmed. "Then Miss Smith has the right of it. I would be quite bereft indeed to miss such a thing."

CHAPTER TWENTY-EIGHT

*N*o gentleman would want her if he ever knew, Aunt Agnes had warned Belle.

No proper lady would ever put on a puppet show for the children of servants and tenants, Harriet adamantly agreed.

Belle had listened but firmly refused to capitulate. Then she'd gone up to her room, changed into her puce dress—it wasn't the most flattering on her, but it provided her arms with the necessary room to move—and then packed her puppets and walked to Easthill Manor. By the time she'd set up everything she would need to perform her little show, she could hear dozens of young children just outside the door.

Lady Wilkins had offered her the use of the small west parlor. It was a cozy room, usually only occupied by family. But with the side table pulled into the center of the room and a cloth draped over the front, Belle had a perfect stage for her puppets. The rug in the center of the room was the most comfortable in all the manor as well, providing the children with a soft place to sit while they watched.

Belle sat on the floor, both legs tucked up close to one side. She closed her eyes, breathing in the emptiness around her. She could hear the children just past the closed doors, but for now, she was the only one in the room.

Slowly she thought through the simple script she'd readied for tonight. There was the princess and her conversation with the jester. That was followed by the jester and the knight. Then the knight would battle the beast of the forest. She would need to remember to include the knight landing many solid blows as the boys especially seemed to enjoy those moments. Then, the knight and the princess would dance.

Her script melted away in her head. Somehow, the prince stopped looking like a simply crafted puppet, and instead smiled at her as James was wont to do. The dance stopped being something her two hands orchestrated and became her standing out on the balcony with James, laughing about their imagined partners.

Belle opened her eyes and pulled her mind back into the present before she could remember what happened next.

She glanced over the puppets across her lap and on the floor beside her. James was gone, and that was that. Her chances of becoming Lady Wilkins were also no more, but she'd been surprised at the dramatic lack of sadness which had followed that change. Instead, she felt mostly happy that her old friend and her new friend were making a match.

She would stay focused on them tonight. Belle felt nothing but joy for them. That, she could hold on to. That and her new hope. She felt confident that though her plans had not come to fruition as she'd always dreamed, something good would come her way. If not, then at least she could be a better person for having gone through it all. That was the basis for her hope now.

Standing, she checked her puppets one last time, and then made her way to the door. She turned the doorknob. Beyond, the children's voices quieted.

Belle opened it slowly to find over three dozen wide eyes

staring eagerly up at her. And to think, at one time she'd canceled the show. What folly that had been. She would always bless James for being the one to speak up and bring her back to her senses.

"Who's ready to see some puppets?" she asked.

The question was met with a resounding cheer. Several of the parents, who stood in an arc around the children, shushed them. Belle only laughed, pulled the door open further, and ushered them all inside.

The puppet show was very well accepted. Though Belle could not see any of the children or parents' faces as she performed, she clearly heard their shrieks of terror at the dragon, their cries of triumph at the knight's valor, and their sighs of happiness at the closing.

In the end, she stood and curtsied as all in the room applauded. The children quickly turned to one another and with giggles and excited tones talked to one another, even as the parents began ushering them back out of the room.

"Thank you, my lady."

Belle turned to find Lily, the young girl she'd met in town just over two months ago looking up at her.

A young boy about her same age stood nearby, leaning over to Lily and whispering, "I don't think she is a lady."

"Of course she is!" Lily stomped as she spoke.

The boy glanced at Belle, clearly hesitant. "But I thought ladies were worried about dresses and lace, not puppets. And my mum called her *Miss*."

Lily pulled her chin up into the air. "Fancy dresses and lace don't make a woman a lady. Being good does."

Belle grew still. Her mother's voice echoed yet again through her mind. *Always a lady*. She'd been so young when last she'd heard those words, and she'd understood them to mean that Belle should always act proper. But suppose her mother had meant something else entirely?

Always a lady. Her mother hadn't meant that Belle needed to prove herself; she'd meant the opposite. Her mother saw Belle as a lady already, lack of title and wealth notwithstanding. She had been instilling in Belle the knowledge that even without those things that society most coveted, Belle was still a lady and, as such, she should still respect herself.

"Isn't that right?" Lily asked her.

Belle dropped to her knees, lowering herself to eye level with the two children. "Most certainly," Belle said, wrapping her arms around the girl.

Lily hugged her back. Oh, if only this wise girl had helped Belle realize as much weeks ago, she could have been spared such heartache and humiliation. Ah, well. What was done was done. Belle could only hope she was a better person for all of it.

A woman behind Belle called to Lily and the young boy and they both followed her out quickly. As they walked away, a young woman with red hair approached Belle. She appeared close to sixteen and was dressed like an abigail.

"Pardon me, miss," the young woman said with a curtsy.

"Yes?" Belle asked.

The young woman glanced about herself, then cleared her throat. "I'm not wanting to be speaking out of turn, only, I thought you might like to know."

Belle waited for another minute while the young woman shifted about before continuing.

"I came tonight because I wanted to see what you looked like."

"What I looked like?"

A quick nod. "After all I heard about you."

Oh, dear. Belle knew there would be talk after she called off the engagement.

"You don't need to worry, miss," the young woman hurried on. "My mistress, she says she never heard of anything so brave as what you did for his lordship and Miss Smith."

Belle stared. It wasn't very ladylike, but she couldn't help herself. "Brave?"

"Oh, yes. And all the other ladies that come to visit all say the same thing. They all have quite a lot of respect for the young lady who let love have a chance."

She never would have expected that. Belle simply didn't know what to say.

The young woman gave her a short curtsy once more. "If I was you, I'd want to know. I hope you won't think ill of me for gossiping like that."

"It is quite all right," Belle said, her voice barely above a whisper.

The young woman left her with a small smile.

Alone in the room once more, Belle closed her eyes and tipped her head back. Good heavens—she had the respect of several of the women in the neighborhood? Who could have imagined such a response?

"That was quite the performance."

Belle's eyes shot open as she whirled around. Not only was she not as alone as she'd believed, but she knew that voice far too well.

"James?"

He stood on the far side of the room in tan breeches and a dark blue superfine. Gracious, but he looked handsome.

Belle felt rooted to the spot, yet he strolled toward her, appearing most unaffected.

"I thought..." She stumbled over the words. "That is, I didn't know you were here."

"I slipped in with the parents."

"No." She smiled. No doubt it was a foolish grin, but she couldn't seem to school her expression just now. "I meant, I didn't know you were *here*, at Easthill Manor."

He moved up beside her, slipping one arm around her waist. "I wasn't. But then I heard that you'd jilted my cousin."

"Oh?" she asked, basking in the alluring warmth his arms provided. "And what is your opinion on the subject?" Not only were her lips refusing to follow decorum, her hands moved up his arms of their own free will.

"I do happen to be quite fond of my cousin. He is an upstanding chap and all that."

"While true, you must give allowance for his lack of humor."

James's lips pulled to the side. "You have me there. Fezzi is known to miss a joke or two."

"And he doesn't dance with me on the balcony."

"He probably doesn't pour flour all over himself either."

Belle tucked herself up closer to him. "Can I tell you a secret? I am quite partial to men all covered in flour."

Slowly he lowered his lips to hers. The kiss was soft and sweet. Still, it ignited something heated and ardent inside her. Belle's fingers tangled themselves up in the bit of hair at the base of his neck.

"If you must know my opinion on the subject, I could not be more overjoyed," James said.

She didn't leave him time to say anything else. Belle went up on her toes and kissed him again, passionately this time. His mouth moved over hers, then trailed along her chin and toward her ear.

"Marry me, my dearest?" he asked.

"Yes," she breathed out. "Most assuredly yes."

He rested his forehead against hers. "I cannot offer you a title or even much wealth. But we will live comfortably, and I promise to always love and cherish you."

"As it turns out," Belle said, "I don't need a title or wealth, after all. *You* are all I could ever hope for and more."

If the kiss James gave her next was any indicator, she was all *he* ever hoped for and more, as well.

EPILOGUE

One Year Later

"Not yet," Belle hissed in as quiet a tone as she could manage while trying not to laugh.

James only pursed his lips and scowled at her.

"The knight has to hit the dragon a few more times *before* he gets mortally wounded."

James sighed but returned his dragon puppet to only wailing at being hit instead of aggressively charging the knight puppet on Belle's hand.

The children laughed—probably perfectly aware of Belle and James's not-completely-hidden discussion behind the blanket. Moreover, this year, the audience included the dowager Lady Wilkins, Fezzi, and the new Lady Wilkins, Georgiana, or "George" as she'd given Belle and James leave to call her.

Earlier that day, Fezzi and George had announced that they, along with the dowager, would soon be traveling to America for a time and wondered if James and Belle wouldn't see to Easthill Manor for them. After they'd agreed, Fezzi had clapped James on the shoulder, saying, "Many a time, I have not wondered but that you would have made a better earl than me."

Belle and James had shared a knowing smile. After all, the earldom truly should have been James's. Still, that Fezzi had it was not something they'd regretted one single day.

Belle had answered for them. "We don't need an earldom to be respected, and we certainly don't need it to be happy."

And she'd meant it.

Belle shifted her weight, getting the next puppet—a woodland nymph—ready for her grand entrance. Heavens, but having them *both* behind the table gave her ever so much less space than she was used to. Belle was quite certain James's legs were sticking out past the edge on one side, and Belle worried her own skirt was sticking out on the other. Still, no one in their young audience seemed to mind.

"All right," Belle whispered. "Now."

James charged his dragon forward, the fabric mouth landing against the knight's chest. Belle feigned her best death-cry and pulled the puppet down below the edge of the table. James was clearly trying to keep quiet, but his laughter set him to shaking and, sitting shoulder to shoulder, Belle was fully aware.

"At least I don't sound like an ox pulling its foot out of the mud," she hissed.

That only made James laugh all the more. They'd practiced playing all the parts, and in the end, they had both believed they each made a better dying cry. But Belle had been at this longer and deemed her opinion as more experienced, and James had finally relented.

The woodland nymph rose up, dipping its fabric hands in a small bowl of short, silk threads and tossing them over the table. The bits of thread caught the light and sparkled as they floated down. Belle sincerely hoped the children were as mesmerized as she'd envisioned—she'd sacrificed one of her favorite ribbons for the "magic" after all.

Sure enough, the children oohed and aahed. The knight arose once more, on James's hand this time, and again waged battle with the fierce dragon. With both attacker and victim on either of James's hands, the battle flowed quite well. The children cried out when the dragon appeared to once more be winning, then cheered as the knight finally stuck his sword through its stomach.

Belle used her free hand to bring up the princess, whom the knight quickly ran over to and kissed.

James leaned over and kissed Belle while everyone was distracted with the happily-ever-after.

As the children cheered the ending, Belle stood and bowed. James was quickly organizing the puppets as several of the children approached the table to say their thank-yous. One young boy in particular was very pleased, and he nearly jumped *onto* the side table in his excitement. The bowl with all the tiny bits of silk ribbon rocked, and then tumbled off the table.

It flipped upside-down as it turned its contents out all over James.

The children stilled, their wide eyes looking over James and the bits of silk all over his hair and shoulders. Belle took one look at the mess and laughed. Soon James and then the children joined in.

Shortly after that, the parents ushered the children from the room, leaving James and Belle alone.

James shook his head as he stood. "Before you, I was quite adept at staying clean. Now, I seem to be forever covered in one thing or another."

Belle shook her head as she began brushing bits of ribbon off his shoulders. "You can't blame me. The messes are always of your own making."

His lovely blue eyes sparkled in the way she'd enjoyed seeing so many times since their wedding. "You keep saying that, yet it never happens unless you're around." He wrapped his arms around her and pulled her up close. "What do you have to say to that, Mrs. Radcliff?"

"I'd say I'm still not tired of being called that."

"I should hope not." James bent down and kissed her.

Belle was certain she could have forgotten everything else and simply melted into his arms. However, she had one other thing planned for tonight.

Pulling back—though James protested slightly—she took hold of his hand. "I haven't given you your Christmas gift yet."

"What do you call those very fine slippers I unwrapped on St. Nicolas Day?"

"Those were your *first* gift." What she'd made for him *before* the doctor had visited.

He chuckled. "Have I told you how adorable you are when uncertain?"

She must have been chewing on her bottom lip again; he was forever calling her out for that, though she knew he honestly rather liked it.

James kissed her, and for a moment, Belle forgot what she'd been about. Then she placed her hands firmly on his chest and pushed back slightly.

"Stop that, or you won't get your next gift," she said, firmly.

"I'm sure it can wait."

Belle laughed. "Not for long, it can't."

He listed his head, his brow dropping in confusion.

Belle took hold of his hand once more, placing it against her stomach.

He only looked all the more confused. Then realization dawned. His mouth dropped open, and his eyes lighted with joy. "Of a truth?"

Belle nodded. "Are you happy?"

James's reply was to wrap her in his arms, picking her up and twirling her around twice before setting her back down and kissing her soundly.

"You, Belle Radcliff," James said, "are undeniably everything I have ever hoped for and more."

"Well," Belle replied, loving the feel of his arms around her, "Christmas is a grand time for hope."

James kissed her on the forehead. "A grand time for hope, indeed."

The End

The series continues in
The Joy of Christmas Present

AFTERWORD

I hope you have enjoyed *The Hope of Christmas Past*. While I only took Charles Dickens's story in essence, I have made many references to the original, particularly to the scenes which transpire during the visit of the first spirit; still, some inspiration also comes from the scenes before the first spirit appears.

Characters:
~Belle was named for the young woman Scrooge once loved, a "dowerless girl." Dickens doesn't tell us much about her, only that she was the one to break the engagement after recognizing that Scrooge had become too greedy, while she continued to value love over money. We also know that she did eventually fall in love with another man, was married, and had several children and a very happy home life.

~Fezziwig is the gentleman whom Scrooge once worked for as a young man. In this story, there is Fezzi, who uses some of the same odd phrases ("Hilli-ho!", "Yo ho", and one of my favorites, "Before a man can say Jack Robinson!"). Though I did make Fezzi younger than Fezziwig was in the original story,

AFTERWORD

this cheerful man who joyfully exclaimed, "No more work tonight. Christmas Eve, Dick. Christmas, Ebenezer!" was the inspiration all the same.

~Of course, Mr. Marley and Mr. Scrooge also walk across the page in this story. However, since they also appear in later books in this series, I will refrain from saying more here.

Scenes:

~There are several scenes which define Scrooge's past. One of the most poignant is when we learn that Scrooge was all but abandoned as a child. He was sent away to school at a very young age and not even allowed to return home for Christmas. I chose to allude to Scrooge's past by making Belle's similar. She, too, was never truly accepted by family and was forever left behind at Christmas.

~While I could find no references to puppets or marionettes in Charles Dickens's story, one of my favorite movie renditions includes a puppeteer who owes Scrooge more than he can pay. That being said, performances on Christmas Day and all during the "jolly holidays" were very common during the Regency and Victorian eras, and the love of performances is referenced by Charles Dickens. When Scrooge first sees himself as a young boy, shut up in the school on Christmas, he sees the other children he knew through the window, all dressed up and acting out a play. Moreover, the image of a puppeteer, working hard to cheer up children while struggling to support himself, has always touched me. So, though a puppet show isn't fully true to Dickens, I added it all the same.

~When Scrooge goes back and revisits his time working for Fezziwig, we learn that the man on the fiddle played "Sir Roger de Coverley," a common Christmas time country dance. Which is why, when Fezzi, Belle, James, and Miss Smith decide to have their own small ball, Fezzi asks Miss Smith to play the same. I reference that same fiddler once more, nearer the end of the story, when James is sitting in a "very public" pub (just before being found by Fezzi and Miss Smith and dragged back to Easthill Manor). During the Regency era, it was not uncommon for a working-class man to have learned to play the fiddle and to bring the instrument with him when he was traveling for work.

~Though I have Fezziwig appear (as Fezzi) in this story, I particularly wanted to draw attention to what Scrooge says about his old employer: "He has the power to render us happy or unhappy; to make our service light or burdensome; a pleasure or a toil ... The happiness he gives, is quite as great as if it cost a fortune." I have always found it telling that Scrooge, even as a young man, did not take responsibility for his own happiness. He blamed his family for shunning him, he claimed Fezziwig had the power to make life enjoyable or not, and later he believed the lie that money could grant him that happiness he'd always found so elusive. This idea was the inspiration for Belle's struggles, and her need to marry Fezzi. In the beginning, she, too, believed all too readily that other people had power over her happiness.

~The last thing Scrooge does while in the presence of the Ghost of Christmas Past is to thrust an extinguisher cap over the spirit, pressing it down hard:

"The spirit dropped beneath it, so that the extinguisher covered its whole form; but though Scrooge pressed down with all his force, he could not hide the light, which streamed from under it, in an unbroken flood upon the ground."

This is echoed in the last glimpse we get of Scrooge in this story, when he considers what Belle has said to him, but, in the end, chooses to extinguish the light rather than accept it. At least, for now.

Phrases:

There are so many wonderful lines in Charles Dickens's

story, I could not help but add several to my own. Some I used verbatim, others I changed slightly to more smoothly fit into the scene. It is my hope that in doing so, readers can better see how this story follows the spirit of the original.

~"Ask me who I *was*." Mr. Jacob Marley; spoken to Scrooge when he first comes to visit.

Echo: when James first meets Mr. Marley and learns he once was a very different man than he is now.

~"You may be an undigested bit of beef, a blot of mustard, a crumb of cheese, a fragment of an underdone potato." Mr. Ebenezer Scrooge; to Marley, by way of explanation as to why he doesn't believe that Marley is a spirit visiting him from beyond the grave.

Echo: As Belle and James are leaving after burning the letter with Mr. Scrooge, Scrooge blames his fever on what he ate.

~"… if it can cheer and comfort you in time to come, as I would have tried to do, I have no just cause to grieve." Belle; opening line as she breaks her engagement with Scrooge.

Echo: Directly after Belle brings James the letter. James calls Belle out on her single-minded ambition to marry for a title, asking her if wealth and title will ever provide cheer and comfort in times to come.

~"This is the even-handed dealing of the world … There is nothing on which it is so hard as poverty; and there is nothing it professes to condemn with such severity as the pursuit of wealth!" Mr. Ebenezer Scrooge; as a young man, speaking to Belle.

Echo: When James first meets with Scrooge, Scrooge asks James why not keep the title for himself; after all, the world is unrelentingly hard on those who are poor.

~"You fear the world too much … I have seen your nobler aspirations fall off one by one, until the master-passion, Gain, engrosses you. Have I not?" Belle; spoken to Scrooge.

Echo: Again, when James is calling Belle out for wanting a title and wealth. Like Scrooge, she had begun to push all other aspirations aside, growing ever more focused on her marriage to Fezzi.

~ "'One shadow more!' exclaimed the Ghost. 'No more!' cried Scrooge ... 'remove me from this place ... I cannot bear it ... haunt me no longer!'"

Echo: After Belle tells her aunt and cousin she is engaged to Fezzi, neither are very happy for her. She is, once again, alone and rejected. Seeing a shadow cast by the fire of the two close together, and herself left out, Belle feels she can no longer stand to be haunted by her past and removes herself from the room.

DISCUSSION QUESTIONS

1. Christmas has meant many different things to many different people throughout history. The Christmas we celebrate today was largely influenced by Charles Dickens's *A Christmas Carol*, first published in 1843. What was your first experience with this often re-told story? A movie, the original book, an adaptation, a theater performance? How did it change the way you think about Christmas? How does it still influence you?
2. Belle was often neglected as a child. She was made to feel unloved and unwanted. This had a large impact on how she went about seeking love as an adult. How has the way you were raised changed your views on love and marriage? Have you had to overcome negative preconceptions? If so, what helped you to do so?
3. In Charles Dickens's story, Scrooge says, "There is nothing on which [the world] is so hard as poverty; and there is nothing it professes to condemn with such severity as the pursuit of wealth!" Do you

believe this contradictory stance on money has changed since the mid 1800's? If so, how? If not, why hasn't it?

4. In this story, Belle learns (as Scrooge does in *A Christmas Carol*) that money does not provide long-standing happiness or comfort. In a world where people seem quick to betray or hurt, it's easy to see why someone might center their trust on money. After all, money cannot betray or purposely hurt anyone. Nonetheless, there is a price to be paid if one chooses to focus solely on gain. What do you think the price is for choosing to hold money over relationships?

5. In *A Christmas Carol*, Scrooge speaks of Fezziwig, saying, "He has the power to render us happy or unhappy; to make our service light or burdensome; a pleasure or a toil…" In what ways do you see society blaming others for their happiness or unhappiness? Have you fallen into this trap yourself? What are the possible drawbacks to blaming others for your happiness? Even when not everything that happens to you is of your own making, what are the benefits to taking ownership of your happiness?

He's been waiting months for her to finally notice him.
Except suddenly, he's not the only one vying for her hand.

Download the short story for free at:
www.LauraRollins.com

ACKNOWLEDGMENTS

No book is ever written without much encouragement and support from any number of people. I am forever thankful to my husband and children, as their patience and love is the reason I get to do this.

Special thanks go to my writing groups, for their advice and help. Also to Jenny Proctor and Emily Poole; without your suggestions and edits this book would not have been half so good.

Lastly, thanks to my Father in Heaven, for giving me a beautiful life and the opportunity to create.

ABOUT THE AUTHOR

Laura Rollins has always loved a heart-melting happily ever after. It didn't matter if the story took place in Regency England, in outer space, beneath the Earth's crust, or in a cobbler's shop, if there was a sweet romance, she would read it.

Life has given her many of her own adventures. Currently she lives in the Rocky Mountains with her best-friend, who is also her husband, and their four beautiful children. She still loves to read books and more books; her favorite types of music are classical, Broadway, and country; she'd rather be hiking the mountains than twiddling her thumbs on the beach; and she's been known to debate with her oldest son over whether Infinity is better categorized as a number or an idea.

You can learn more about her and her books, as well as pick up a free story, at:

www.LauraRollins.com

Made in the USA
Monee, IL
18 December 2023